W9-BUN-872

Alien Feast

CHRONiCLES of the FiRST INVASiON • Book One

Alien Feast

MICHAEL SIMMONS
Illustrations by GEORGE O'CONNOR

RB

A NEAL PORTER BOOK
ROARING BROOK PRESS
NEW YORK

The author wishes to thank Simon Boughton, Thaddeus Bower, Anne Dahlie, Elizabeth Dahlie, Susan Dahlie, Gary Goldberger, Emily Hazel, Kathrin Kollmann, Allison Lynn, Victoria Marini, Christopher Miller, George Nicholson, Neal Porter, and Paul Rodeen.

A Neal Porter Book
Published by Roaring Brook Press
Roaring Brook Press is a division of Holtzbrinck Publishing Holdings
Limited Partnership
175 Fifth Avenue, New York, New York 10010
www.roaringbrookpress.com

Distributed in Canada by H.B. Fenn and Company, Ltd.

Library of Congress Cataloging-in-Publication Data
Simmons, Michael, 1970-
Alien feast / Michael Simmons ; illustrated by George O'Connor. – 1st ed.
p. cm.
Summary: In 2017, human-eating aliens have kidnapped two scientists who might cure the disease that is destroying them, and twelve-year-old William Aitkin, his elderly, ailing Uncle Maynard, and the scientists' daughter, Sophie, set out to rescue them.
ISBN-13: 978-1-59643-281-9 ISBN-10: 1-59643-281-0
[1. Extraterrestrial beings–Fiction. 2. Uncles–Fiction. 3. Sick–Fiction. 4. Kidnapping–Fiction. 5. Orphans–Fiction. 6. Science fiction.]
I. O'Connor, George, ill. II. Title. PZ7.D5158Ali 2008 [Fic]–dc22 2007044050

Roaring Brook Press books are available for special promotions and premiums.
For details, contact: Director of Special Markets, Holtzbrick Publishers

Book design by Jennifer Browne
First Edition May 2009
Printed in March 2009 in the United States of America by RR Donnelley Company, Harrisonburg, Virginia
10 9 8 7 6 5 4 3 2 1

For Allison

i

On the twenty-ninth of September, in the year 2017, William Aitkin's so-called stepparents were eaten by aliens, which he didn't particularly mind, seeing as they had never been very nice to him. He was, in fact, greatly relieved to be rid of them since he had always felt that they were standing between him and his dream of becoming a famous violin player. Of course, in a world now overrun by a colony of man-eating aliens, there were quite a few things that would interfere with this dream. But even these hurdles would eventually be overcome.

The fact is that aliens are not quite as smart as you'd think. These aliens in particular did not quite do the planning they should have. And while humans were largely defenseless against their various ray guns and laser bombs, these particular aliens were very susceptible to a specific but initially mysterious virus that existed on Planet Earth. And after wiping out much of modern society, these aliens suddenly became extremely ill, and following a period of terrible suffering (which filled even William with some pity, despite the fact that they had eaten half of humanity), many of them suddenly died, freeing Planet Earth from their total domination but leaving it very different from how they had found it.

The world was different for two main reasons. First, although many of the aliens did die, *many* is not the same as *all*, which means that some aliens also remained. They were highly dangerous, entirely hostile to humans, and strong enough in number to cause very many problems for the people who survived. Still, they hadn't taken over the world entirely. And given the circumstances, they were very preoccupied with curing themselves and getting off the planet, neither of which were easy tasks given their now greatly reduced number. (See chapter six for a broader explanation of this matter.)

Second, because of the method of the alien invasion (again, see chapter six for details), much of the planet was basically destroyed. Many roads, radio towers, large cities, cable television stations, airstrips, grocery stores, and many, many more things were either entirely gone or mostly gone. And the people who lived in or near these places (or were shopping in these grocery stores or driving on these roads) vanished into the wide ether as well.

So, obviously, the world was changed quite a bit. And much of the decades that followed what historians would eventually call the First Invasion was spent struggling to create a new way of life on Planet Earth. And for William in particular, whose stepparents had been mercilessly eaten on a bright fall morning in the year 2017, it would mean the start of a fairly unusual set of adventures.

2

On the day his stepparents were eaten, William was at the Temporary Emergency Center getting batteries, bread, cold cuts, and bottled water. His stepparents had sent him on this errand because they were too afraid to go out of the house themselves. They lived in the city of Willoughby, and alien sightings had been reported in town for the previous several days. William didn't really want to go to the store, seeing that he didn't want to get eaten by an alien any more than his stepparents did. But, again, his stepparents were not very thoughtful people. They decided that if anyone should get eaten, it ought to be William.

"Why should we go when we have the boy!" his stepfather yelled over and over that morning.

It's worth noting at this point that having two stepparents is a fairly unusual arrangement. It's almost unheard of, to be honest, although there is a reasonable explanation. William's real mother died when he was five. His father remarried, and then died himself when William was eight. His stepmother then remarried when William was ten (two years before the aliens invaded), and this is the man William would eventually come to know as his stepfather.

It should also be pointed out here that stepparents can often be wonderful people, as William well knew. His stepparents, however, were very far from being wonderful. They never gave him enough food. They were always complaining about the nuisance of having a young boy wandering around their home. And they despised his violin playing. Worst of all, in the midst of one of the greatest catastrophes in the history of the earth, they repeatedly put William in danger (for the water and the cold cuts and the bread and the batteries) rather than face the danger themselves. And this is why it was somewhat ironic when William returned with a small red wagon loaded up with provisions to discover that aliens had come by, chased his stepparents around his house, and then, apparently, eaten them.

William knew his stepparents had been eaten because he found their feet, bitten off at the ankle, lying in the middle of his living room. By this time (it was now nearly two months since the aliens first invaded) it was well known among human beings that aliens did not like to eat feet. This, in fact, was something that William always found puzzling. Aliens were not picky about any of the other body parts. They'd eat things like hair and eyeballs without thinking twice. But feet were repulsive to them. Generally speaking, feet were repulsive to William as well, but then this wasn't really an issue since he was never going around trying to eat anyone.

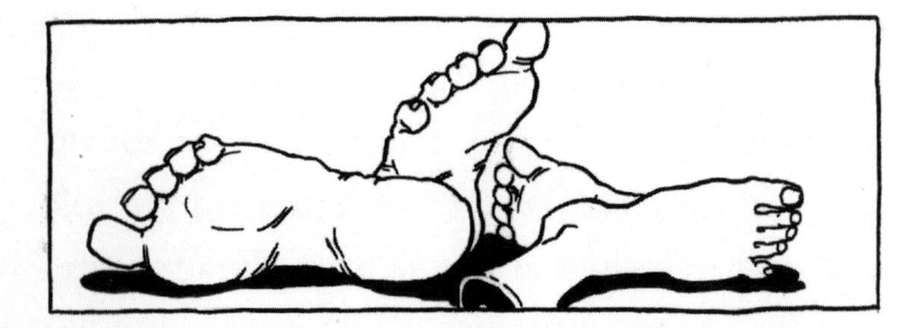

Still, as he stood in his living room, calculating what must have happened, another matter quickly came to mind–one that took his attention away from the question of why aliens did not like to eat feet. It seemed likely that there might be aliens still lurking about, and that he ought to figure out a way to get himself to safety.

"I think I need to get out of here," William finally said to himself as he looked at the four feet of his stepparents.

He thought for a moment, then grabbed his stepfather's car keys, which sat on the entryway table. William had an uncle he could turn to for help–one Uncle Maynard (from his mother's side), a world-famous composer and also William's violin teacher. Uncle Maynard was the person William was closest to in the world, and William quickly decided that he would drive to his house.

Now, technically speaking, William was not allowed to drive a car. He was too young and he had no driver's license. It was entirely against the law, in fact. But, technically speaking, most notions of law were rapidly fading away. Many of the police officers had been eaten. Many of the judges had been eaten. And even the people on the television shows about police officers and judges had been eaten. So it was quite unlikely that William would be arrested.

After packing a few items into a small bag (including clothes for a few days, several sandwiches, and his violin), he ran out to the driveway and jumped into the car.

3

William had always faced a certain kind of problem. He was not a very good student. He was a magnificent violin player and learned music very quickly. But he did very poorly in school. The reasons for this were a mystery to everyone, including William, who tended to feel that he was particularly brilliant. But it was true that he did not like to study and rarely did his homework, and this made the teachers at his very strict school furious.

William had seen numerous school psychologists, learning experts, and special teachers about his various educational problems. His explanation was always that he found everything besides his violin to be extremely tedious.

"Everything else is just so boring," he once told a short, bearded man who asked him why he never did his homework.

Still, William could never quite escape a kind of tiny, lingering suspicion that maybe he wasn't as bright as he imagined he was. And as William sat in the front seat of the car, he suffered the kind of crippling lack of self-confidence that he often felt in school when he was bewildered by a teacher's question or a more formal exam. Despite the fact that there was now no real law preventing him from driving, he actually did not really know how to do it. He had seen it done before–millions of times. But seeing something done and actually doing it are very different things.

Still, this was no time for self-doubt. After finding the keyhole (commonly called the ignition), he started the engine, moved a large handle (commonly called the gear shift), stepped down on the gas pedal, and began backing out of the driveway.

In some ways, it was all rather easy. He just pointed the car with the steering wheel and stepped on the gas. But gas pedals can be tricky things to operate. And as William reached the end of the driveway, the engine suddenly roared and he shot across the road, over the opposite curb, and into a large bush in his neighbor's front yard. Fortunately, though, not too much damage was done. There was another large pedal that operated the brake, and William worked this pedal with remarkable talent.

Only a bush, William thought. *That was lucky.*

William looked around for a second. He took several deep breaths. Then he pushed the gear shift forward and looked down the street to make sure no other cars were coming toward him. It would probably be best if he didn't hit anything else. William did wonder, though, if he could really drive to his uncle's without hurting himself.

And then he looked across the street and suddenly wondered if he'd ever return to his house again. It was a difficult question. He had been very unhappy there in recent years. Given that, he was more than glad to leave. But it hadn't been all bad–not when his parents were alive. And although his parents had been dead for many years, William could still remember in vivid detail scenes of his mother doing things like making him huge pancake breakfasts and his father happily listening to him play the violin. It was a very difficult thing to think about, leaving home like this. But all at once he heard a strange whistling sound. It was one of the aliens' aircraft. William decided that perhaps he ought to get moving. He didn't see the aircraft. And it might not even have been that close. But William wisely concluded that he ought to ponder the ways in which his life was now changed once he was a bit more safe.

He took his foot off the brake, stepped on the gas pedal, and felt the car lurch forward. In the next instant he was barreling crookedly down the street and beginning the journey to the other side of the city and the house of his uncle.

4

It should be pointed out that Willoughby was a medium-sized town, and in many ways it was not the kind of place one would imagine aliens would invade. There were bigger cities filled with more people that might make for better places to carry out a conquest of Planet Earth. But the aliens seemed to be invading everywhere in those days. And, in truth, there was one thing (at this point in the history of the First Invasion) that did make Willoughby particularly appealing to the invaders, seeing that most of them were now dying from a mysterious illness: Willoughby was built around an enormous and extremely important university, called the University of Willoughby, which was famous for its school of medicine and its study of diseases. There were numerous famous doctors there who had found the cures to countless illnesses that had long plagued Planet

Earth. Specifically (and relevant to this story) there were two particular doctors who had come up with more cures for terrible diseases than anyone else alive. They were a husband-and-wife team, and their names were Doctors Vladimir and Lena Astronovitch.

All this is important for you to know because they were the parents of one Sophie Astronovitch, who happened to be sitting on a curb as William was speedily weaving by in his stepfather's car. In fact, when he saw her he screeched to a halt, very surprised to see her sitting at the side of the street, given the current situation and how dangerous it was to be outside.

"Sophie, what are you doing out here?" William called from his now open car window. "The aliens are everywhere. You can't be out on the street."

"I don't care," Sophie replied, slowly looking up. "The aliens took my parents away."

William could now see that Sophie's eyes were red, and that she had probably been crying for a long time. Her voice was scratchy, her hair was messed up, and she looked extremely anxious.

William thought about what she said for a

moment and then finally asked, "Do you mean they *ate* your parents?"

"No," she replied. "They didn't eat them. They took them away. I watched them do it. I was hiding in the downstairs hallway."

This was puzzling to William, and he didn't quite know what to say. "Are you sure?" he said.

Sophie gave William an angry stare. William paused for another moment, then said, "Maybe you should come with me then. I'm going to visit my uncle. He might know what to do." William hesitated, and then said, "My stepparents were just eaten. I don't think we have much time to wait around."

Sophie continued to stare angrily, when noise from one of the alien aircraft once again sounded in the distance. Sophie tried to keep up her angry stare, but it soon gave way to more of a frightened one, and in the next instant, she was off the curb and getting into William's car.

"I didn't know you knew how to drive," she said, shutting the door behind her.

"I'm extremely good at all sorts of things," William replied, and then quickly regretted it, thinking that this was a fairly stupid thing to say. By this point in his life, William knew full well that young women rarely like braggarts. And the fact was, (and this is also very important for you to know) Sophie was not any ordinary person in William's life. William had known Sophie since he was three, and his feelings for her seemed to change from year to year. He spent much of his early childhood liking her a great deal, and he played with her on a regular basis from nursery school through third grade. By the time they were in fourth grade, however, William despised Sophie for reasons even he could not really understand. This lasted for two years, until the end of fifth grade, when William found that he suddenly liked her a great deal again, but was so confused by this fact that it simply drove him to play the violin with greater daring and enthusiasm. In fact, William's violin playing reached new and great levels during this period. And as William again stepped down on the gas pedal, and began driving off to the other side of town, he suddenly wished that he was now alone in his attic so he could spend the afternoon playing violent violin pieces written by dead Austrian composers.

5

The drive to Uncle Maynard's house took fifteen minutes, and since meeting Uncle Maynard for the first time always led to some pandemonium (William was now thinking exactly this as he looked over at Sophie), it seems that this is probably a good time to talk a little more about this man.

Uncle Maynard was in his mid-seventies, very tall, somewhat thin, and had bushy gray hair that he either never combed or that he combed often, but to no good effect. He had an odd but appealing look to him, and fifty years earlier he had been thought of as quite a dashing young man around the city of Willoughby. Despite his pleasant appearance, however, Uncle Maynard also seemed slightly odd to the people who met him. His eyes darted about as he talked. He moved his hands wildly as he spoke. He tended to make very inappropriate comments. And he had a voice that could go from shrill heights to bellowing depths in the time it took him to say a single word.

Uncle Maynard also had a terrible heart condition, and always claimed to be "very nearly dead" when he talked to William about the world and his future.

"I'm just about dead, William," he used to say, often when they were taking a break from his violin lessons. "I'm very nearly dead, and soon I'll be gone from this world, and you'll have to carry on without me."

And this is, in fact, something that William pointed out to Sophie. "My uncle might talk a lot about his heart when you meet him," he said, weaving to avoid a large branch in the road. "And dying. He talks a lot about dying. It's pretty much his favorite subject."

The thing was that this obsession with his heart didn't always seem entirely believable to William, seeing that Uncle Maynard had been talking about his impending death for as long as William could remember. All the same, it was always unsettling to hear, as it usually is when someone talks about his own death.

And the fact was that Uncle Maynard had suffered several heart attacks in the past. And he took over twenty pills a day. "This is all that's keeping me alive, my boy!" Uncle Maynard often said. "If it weren't for this, I'd be on the floor, completely unable to breathe, probably dying right before your very eyes." And it was also true that in the past year, he had seemed quite a bit weaker. So Uncle Maynard's grim predictions about his coming death might well have been right, although for the many years he had been making them, they never came true.

In general, Uncle Maynard was known by most people in the city of Willoughby as a bit standoffish and a bit miserly, neither of which really applied to him in any kind of true sense. He was indeed rich, having spent a lifetime composing extremely popular music that was played all over the world. And he lived in an enormous house, filled with lots of rooms that even William had never been in. But Uncle Maynard never seemed to mind spending his money, most of which went to buying antique musical instruments, sheet music, and the various strange salted and cured foods that he ordered from far-off places.

It was also true that Uncle Maynard wasn't always as friendly as he should be, although William found that Uncle Maynard did have lots of friends and liked people quite a bit. He was just a bit suspicious of strangers. But Uncle Maynard was a very kind man. This was true. And over the years he had been better to William than any other person in his life. Despite all of Uncle Maynard's so-called prickliness, and his tendency to often say the wrong thing, there was no one that William cared about or trusted more.

Finally, Uncle Maynard was terrified of robbers and murderers (as perhaps we all are to some degree). He had built an elaborate security system for his mansion, including ten well-trained German shepherd dogs that roamed the grounds. There was also a huge stone wall surrounding the mansion, with an enormous iron gate at the entrance to the driveway. And it is, in fact, at this enormous gate, that our two friends (following ten more minutes of erratic and extremely hazardous driving) eventually arrived.

"This is it!" William announced, as they came to a fairly abrupt stop about three inches from the gate's twisting iron bars.

"I'm not sure I want to go in," Sophie said, looking a bit frightened by this strange, dark house.

"It's great in there," William said. "My uncle is just a little odd. But I'm sure you'll like him."

Sophie stared up at the large, dark house again and looked like she had more to say on the matter. But she kept quiet, because, after all, what was she going to do at this point?

William then rolled down the window and pressed a red button that stuck out of a large steel speaker at the side of a towering stone column. In a few seconds, a video camera mounted high on the gate turned and pointed at the car. There was a pause, and then William heard, "Go away!" from the speaker.

William yelled back to the speaker, "Uncle Maynard. It's me, William."

The lens on the video camera began to get longer, zooming in on the car's front window.

After a short pause, William heard, "What are you doing driving a car? I'm not sure that's something you're allowed to do."

"My stepparents have been eaten by the aliens,"

William said. “I had to leave. It’s not safe for me to be at home anymore.”

There was a pause.

“Are you sure?”

“I found their feet.”

“Goodness me!” There was another brief pause, and then the gate abruptly swung back. William looked over at Sophie, and then began jerkily guiding the car up the driveway.

It took two minutes or so to make it up to the house. And after parking, and walking through the broad rock garden set at the front of Uncle Maynard’s mansion, Sophie and William arrived at the front door and pushed the doorbell.

In another second, they heard a series of clacking noises–Uncle Maynard unlocking the various locks that secured his door–and before long, the large oak door swung open. There was no one visible at first, but then, from behind the door, stepped a very weary and slightly confused-looking Uncle Maynard. He had a wool cap on, a long blue scarf wrapped around his neck, and a thermometer clenched in his mouth.

“Mmmf gggsddds!” he said, and then, after

looking slightly agitated, took the thermometer out of his mouth. "My goodness!" he said, now more clearly. "What astonishing news! What times we're living in!" He looked at the thermometer, shook his head, and then said, "I'm afraid you've come at a very bad time though, as I seem to have caught something. I'm extremely sick. All the same, I'm very glad you've made it."

"Are you drinking lots of tea?" William said. Uncle Maynard was an obsessive tea drinker, and believed that all good conversations began with the suggestion that one ought to drink more of it.

"I've had about three pots today," he replied. "And just right now, I'm brewing a fourth, which I'll be delighted to share with you. But come in! Come in! I think it's not a good idea to be standing around outside."

Uncle Maynard led them into the house and proceeded to relock all of the locks on the front door. Then he typed codes into two alarm panels in the entry hall. Again, Uncle Maynard was terrified of burglars, con men, wild animals, delinquent neighborhood boys, and any number of other things that might want to get hold of him.

As for whether his security measures might keep out the aliens, this was another question. But by this point in the history of the First Invasion, it was well established that these particular aliens were extremely lazy, and while they might have been able to get past Uncle Maynard's security, it would have been quite a bit of trouble, especially if all they were going to get to eat was a skinny old man and two young people–not the kind of meal that these particular aliens liked very much. And there was one other thing. For reasons still unknown, the aliens were absolutely terrified of dogs.

In any event, Uncle Maynard finished typing in his codes, said, "We should be safe now," then paused, looked at his thermometer again, and said (staring at Sophie), "Who are you?"

Sophie stumbled on her words but finally managed to say, "I'm a friend of William's."

"And why are you here? Did your parents get eaten as well?"

Sophie looked totally stone-faced, and then, without warning, suddenly burst into tears. This surprised William, because Sophie was always so tough. But having your parents get eaten is more than even the toughest can bear, and the only thing that managed to calm Sophie down was William saying over and over, "They've been kidnapped! They haven't been eaten! They've been kidnapped!"

Uncle Maynard looked confused, but then apologized to Sophie, saying, "I'm so, so sorry. I think I put that rather badly. I'm very sorry."

Eventually Sophie's crying slowed, and then she said she would be all right. "I'm okay," she said. "I'm sorry."

"No, I'm sorry," Uncle Maynard said again. "I really am. I'm afraid I never know quite how to behave around other people." He then tucked his thermometer into the front pocket of his thick cardigan sweater, wrapped his scarf tightly around his neck, and said, "I need something hot to drink because I'm beginning to get cold. I think you both ought to join me. This way!" He then turned and walked toward the kitchen. After a moment of hesitation, William and Sophie followed.

6

And since we're now in a sort of mode of introduction (having just met Uncle Maynard, after all) there are just a few other things you will need to know. As follows:

THE ALIENS

It was widely accepted that the particular aliens that conducted the First Invasion behaved very oddly. This, of course, makes sense, seeing that they were aliens. But they were odd in ways that no one ever imagined aliens might be. If they were able to fly halfway across the galaxy, for instance, you'd think that they'd have to be a species of supergeniuses. But these aliens did not appear to be supergeniuses at all. In fact, they were more like a pack of rowdy six-year-olds at a birthday party. They simply ran around Earth, eating and breaking things, and they would often even start fighting with each other. It was not unusual, for instance, to see aliens locked in wrestling holds, beating each other over the head, snarling angrily in each other's faces, and even shooting each other with their electric guns–although the guns were usually set on low power so they didn't actually kill each other.

It was once suggested on a television show that these aliens might, in fact, be delinquent teenagers. The announcer said, "We may very well be at the mercy of a rabble of alien teenage delinquents." It was an interesting theory, but this particular announcer was eaten shortly after making this comment, and no one ever really thought much more about it.

Upon seeing the aliens, the first impression one had was that many comic-book artists and moviemakers had been remarkably insightful when they were first imagining alien life. It was almost as if these various artists had maybe even seen one or two of these creatures before bringing them to life in their artwork. The aliens were ugly, green-skinned things, with long arms, slimy tentacles, a large mouth with razor-sharp teeth, and spindly little legs over which they wore flexible metallic robotic leggings, which helped make up for their lower-body weakness. Their eyes stood up on their heads, almost like hands holding tennis balls, and numbered at least three, although sometimes they had as many as four or five. They also had several small holes in the front of their face, which William imagined worked as something like a nose, and small green ears that looked like broccoli–a food that William abhored. And the aliens were tall–nearly ten feet with their robotic legs–and they were entirely hairless, which only added to their horrible appearance.

It was actually somewhat hard to observe an alien, although they were occasionally on television when they first arrived. They didn't particularly like to be scrutinized by humans and didn't give you much warning that they were around. Of course, if you happened to be one of the unlucky people to get eaten, you probably got a very good sense of what they looked like. Otherwise, you depended on the brief glimpses you caught on TV and in the few newspapers that were still available.

The aliens were also susceptible to many of the normal dangers that afflict human beings. For instance, they could be killed or injured with a bullet, which meant that they weren't entirely immune from human attacks. Because so many of them began dying unexpectedly, they lost some of their weapons, and so they were also vulnerable to attacks from the high-tech alien guns people had taken from them. Still, since they were ten feet tall and always had plenty of firepower at their disposal, they pretty much won most of the battles they had with people.

At first, no one was really sure who they were or what they wanted. They didn't send an advance team of negotiators to announce their intentions. No one even knew they were coming till the day they arrived. And when they did arrive, they started eating everyone, so there wasn't much opportunity to sit down and have a chat about their plans for the future and what, exactly, they wanted on Planet Earth.

Years later, the following would be discovered about these particular aliens: they were a sort of nomadic species who didn't really have a home anywhere, and who went from place to place eating whatever (or whomever) they found along the way, getting supplies to power their fleet of spaceships (uranium and plutonium, most importantly), and then moving on. They were also very, very old–not teenagers at all–and had been at this for quite a long time.

It was also clear that much of the technology they possessed had been taken from other aliens, who were, in fact, supergeniuses. And because of this, they seemed to operate their various aircraft and spaceships and other mysterious devices without a firm grasp of how, exactly, they worked, or how to use them properly. On the few occasions that people spotted aliens operating one or other of their numerous machines, it seemed that they pushed buttons randomly, adjusted levers with no sense of what they were doing, and often banged their guns and machines with their large green fists in bursts of frustration and anger. They were not quick learners, as it were. For instance, while they had somehow mastered the intricacies of space travel, they were entirely confused by things like doorknobs, vending machines, peanut butter jars, and numerous other commonplace items on Planet Earth.

All the same, as stupid as these aliens occasionally seemed, they obviously had some sort of brain power and managed fairly well, seeing that they took over the earth. And they were truly greedy and evil beings, which are qualities that go a very long way when you're trying to conquer a planet.

THE INVASION

In fact, what would become the invasion did not start out as an invasion at all, but was instead a sort of cosmic catastrophe. One evening in early August in the year 2017, the sky was lit up by what seemed to be a long string of beautiful (but not at all normal) stars. These stars, however, were moving, and at a very rapid pace. And by the time everyone began noticing them in the sky, astronomers and astrophysicists were coming on the television to explain to people that a very unexpected and very dangerous thing was about to happen. This beautiful (and some might say peaceful and picturesque) string of stars was, in fact, a strangely aligned series of asteroids that was headed straight for Planet Earth. There was no telling where, exactly, the asteroids would strike, but they would indeed strike the earth–that was certain–and the effects would be astonishing.

"And by astonishing, I mean something very, very bad," one astronomer-newscaster said.

In the next several days, the earth was struck by countless of these asteroids, many of them falling on the planet's large cities, military bases, palaces of kings, homes of presidents, etc.

It was an unimaginable disaster and caused a great deal of trouble for the human race. And as everyone was trying to figure out what had happened, and what to do next, people suddenly started reporting unusual lights darting around in the sky. And then people started noticing strange green aliens who were going around eating people. And although everyone was still confused about the exact details of what was happening, it was now fairly definite that some kind of alien invasion was under way.

So the world was in chaos. And the people who were still alive were left to carry on as best they could. Not everything had been destroyed. Not all the leaders and armies and police forces had been wiped out. Additionally, there was some attempt to organize the remaining people, although it was not very successful. But then, as was actually once predicted in a certain important piece of speculative fiction from the end of the nineteenth century, the aliens started getting sick. The disease quickly spread, and aliens suddenly started having a harder time of it, seeing that most of them were now covered in red spots and vomiting a sort of horrible green alien vomit to the point that they'd simply vomit themselves to death. They were still causing numerous problems, of course (it was during this period that William's stepparents were eaten). Some aliens recovered, and others seemed to be immune to the disease.

All the same, humans began to get a bit more of a foothold. They began to take back some of what was, after all, their own planet. And about this time, about five hundred miles north of Willoughby, there arose a kind of human outpost that was being called the Northern Empire. They were broadcasting messages from their newly established center–the large mining city of Kesselton–and were doing their best to encourage those humans who were still alive to brave the destroyed roads and alien patrols and come to the new settlement to help prepare to fight back. It was an appealing offer to almost everyone in Willoughby, but the journey was treacherous and constituted a great risk. And for people like William's stepparents (who were fairly incompetent), and older people with heart conditions (like Uncle Maynard), and young people who were very nice but generally confused (William), such a journey–at that moment in time–seemed like something of an impossibility.

FURTHER NOTES ABOUT WILLIAM AND SOPHIE

First, what they looked like.

Sophie was athletic, dark haired, blue eyed, and always had a smirk on her face. She was an inch taller than William (a fact he found almost unbearable) and was capable of running at great speeds, as William witnessed numerous times on their school's sports fields. Additionally, Sophie was a magnificent dresser, which seemed to stem less from a sense of fashion and more from the absolute confidence with which she wore whatever suited her on any given day. In

fact, this kind of confidence underpinned everything she did, and whether she was wearing a baseball cap or chewing on a pencil, she had a kind of captivating and self-possessed quality that made young men like William extremely nervous.

William had light-brown hair, clear skin, and generally appealing green eyes. He had a kind of quiet and bookish manner, which seemed to call for a pair of thin, wire-rimmed glasses. But his eyesight had always been first-rate, and he had never needed them–much to his disappointment. He was not short (although he was not quite as tall as Sophie), and he, too, had a kind of athletic air to him. But he didn't care much for sports, for reasons he could never quite explain. In the years that would follow the opening period of the First Invasion, William would be widely regarded as a reasonably handsome person. But at this point in time, it would be most accurate to describe his appearance as (at best) mostly pleasing.

William got along with most people–most of his schoolmates liked him, in fact–but he was also something of a loner. Since school was such a troubling experience (again, he was always getting yelled at or slapped for one thing or another), he didn't really develop too many friends in the schoolyard. His favorite person to spend time with was his uncle. Otherwise, William often kept to himself, preferring music to the company of people.

It should be said, though, that while William did like the company of Sophie, Sophie did not always appear to like the company of William. She was what they call *extremely fickle*, sometimes sitting next to him at lunch and other times refusing to even say hello to him. But this kind of behavior was not at all unusual with Sophie. She was something of a troublemaker herself and seemed to behave in fickle ways with almost everyone. But she was so smart and so charming that she managed to get away with everything. Again, she went to the same strict school as William. They were even in the same grade. But the angry teachers who tormented William did nothing but heap praise on Sophie. In fact, it would not be untrue to say that everyone heaped praise on Sophie.

Additionally, one of Sophie's particular personality traits (although it was something best seen before her parents were taken away) was that she was very sarcastic and very funny, and she often poked fun at the people around her. It was friendly teasing. Mostly. But nervous boys like William tended to dissolve into anxious confusion when she would, for instance, laugh at their clothing or joke about their hair or make remarks about their poor grades. And you can be certain that the sort of anxiousness that Sophie provoked was much on William's mind on that strange day that his stepparents were eaten and he brought Sophie to his uncle's house.

Finally, one of the more important things you need to know, and something only relevant to William: he had an older brother, who was now very far away. His older brother (named Christopher) had always argued bitterly with his stepmother, and when she made the decision to remarry after their father died–then, two years before anyone had even seen an alien–he ran away to live in the coastal city of Great Harbor, nearly fifteen hundred miles away. William himself had thought about running away to join his brother. But he wasn't really old enough, and he knew the police would find him and bring him back. His brother was sixteen when his new stepfather entered their lives, and at sixteen you are allowed to make many decisions for yourself. William was only ten when his stepparents married, and at ten, you pretty much have to do whatever you're told.

Oddly enough, William's brother had spent much of his youth fantasizing about encounters with aliens. He was fascinated by outer space and spent most of his time staring into the heavens with a telescope his father had bought him. And when his father first got sick, now years after the boys' mother had died, he spent more and more of his time gazing into the wide-open sky, looking for planets or stars or possibly visitors from outer space heading toward the earth.

In the aftermath of the invasion, William wondered what his brother thought of the strange new situation humans found themselves in. Being eaten, after all, is probably not what boys think of when they dream about black holes and far-off galaxies. But William had not communicated with his brother since the aliens had first arrived, seeing that many of the world's telecommunications satellites had been shot to pieces by the alien spaceships, and there wasn't anything like a reliable postal service anymore.

As far as William was concerned, this, in fact, was the worst thing about the aliens' arrival. His brother had been gone for two years, but before the invasion, they still talked to each other with some frequency. Now, William didn't even know if his brother was still alive. And although he found it very difficult to even think about whether or not his brother might be dead, the question of his brother's health and safety still occupied much of his thoughts because there weren't that many people in the world that William was close to. This is perhaps one of the most important things for you to know to understand William's story.

7

The provisional and emergency television news was particularly important in those days, seeing that it was one of the few things that could alert you to, say, a band of aliens arriving in your neighborhood in order to eat everyone. It was true that many of the television stations had been destroyed. But there were still a few cable links and a few stations that broadcast over the airwaves. Most towns also had some sort of emergency transmitter to send out various bits of important community information (where to buy bread, how to avoid aliens, etc.). And it is for this reason that Uncle Maynard (who ordinarily despised television) decided that they would turn it on as they were having their tea.

"These aliens are forcing me to watch television," he said, shaking his head as he studied the remote and searched for the on button. "After eating people, it's one of the worst effects they've had on our society."

William nodded in agreement, although he, in fact, liked television a great deal.

The three of them were seated in large split-cane chairs around an enormous table in Uncle Maynard's kitchen. The cavernous room was actually more than a kitchen, and rather like a kind of all-purpose living room, where Uncle Maynard cooked, mended his clothes, played his violin, read novels, and (when forced to by dire situations caused by aliens) watched television.

When Uncle Maynard finally figured out the remote, he switched the television on, and the three stared at a strange collage of patriotic pictures, with patriotic music playing in the background. Uncle Maynard shook his head at the television again, put down the remote, and looked over at the teapot. "Thank goodness, the tea is ready," he said.

Uncle Maynard began to pour out cups of tea, when the patriotic music on the television suddenly halted, and a man with a deep voice began to speak.

"Please pay attention to the following announcement," the man said. "This evening our mayor will deliver an important message on the future of our town. Citizens of Willoughby are instructed to tune in at exactly eight p.m. Thank you."

William looked over at Uncle Maynard, who was rolling his eyes. Uncle Maynard had known the mayor for years, having been good friends with his father, and having taught him to play the violin many years earlier. His opinion of the mayor was not at all favorable. Finally, Uncle Maynard just let out a sigh, turned to the young people, and said, "Now, why don't you tell me more about what happened to you."

Sophie looked very uncomfortable, so William decided that perhaps he ought to begin. He told Uncle Maynard about going to get supplies with his wagon, about returning to find only the feet of his stepparents, about taking his stepfather's car ("Which is more difficult to drive than you'd think," he said). And then he explained how he found Sophie sitting at the side of the road.

Uncle Maynard listened patiently, the whole time saying, "What a terrible thing!" over and over. William knew, however, that his uncle was no less happy than he was about the sudden loss of his stepparents. It was true that William (and probably his uncle) felt bad that they had been eaten. Still, they were such horrible people that William (and probably Uncle Maynard) couldn't help but be somewhat relieved.

After William's story was finished, Uncle Maynard paused for a moment, then looked at Sophie, who was sitting in an uncomfortable and rigid position and now not touching her tea.

"And what about you, Sophie?" Uncle Maynard asked. "Can you tell me what happened?"

"I'm not sure I can," she said, now looking like she was going to burst into tears again.

"Anything you can say would be good. I might be able to help you."

Sophie looked up at Uncle Maynard. But still she hesitated. Then, finally, she took a big gulp of tea, then a very deep breath, and began to tell her story.

Apparently, Sophie had been in the kitchen eating toast and soft-boiled eggs when there was a loud knock on the door. Her parents were in the front sitting room, and they got up and answered it. Sophie also got up to see who it was, but by the time she made it into the hallway, the aliens were already inside the door and had cornered her parents. They were some distance away, and she instantly stopped before they saw her. She crouched just beyond a corner in the hallway and peered around the wall to watch what happened.

There was also a man with the aliens, who stepped forward and, after pausing a moment to take in the surroundings, asked, "Are you Doctor and Doctor Astronovitch of the university's infectious diseases department?"

"Yes," they replied.

The man squinted at them, and then said in what Sophie found to be a particularly terrifying voice, "You have a choice. You can come with me, or you can be eaten by my associates here."

Sophie's parents looked at each other, and then at the aliens, and then at the man, and Vladimir Astronovitch finally said, "I think we'll go with you."

Sophie took a sip of her tea, then looked at Uncle Maynard and William. "I don't think my parents came back to the kitchen for me because they thought I might get eaten," she said.

"I'm sure they wanted you to escape," Uncle

Maynard agreed, putting his large hand on Sophie's shoulder. "I'm sure they left you behind to keep you safe."

Uncle Maynard paused, then said, "You know, I've met your parents–the Doctors Astronovitch. At the university. They've been to my recitals. And I've met them at university parties. They're charming people. And extremely smart. I'm sure the aliens took them because they're useful to them. Maybe they think they'll be able to cure this disease they've got. In which case, they'll surely be kept alive. They won't be eaten. And that means we'll be able to find them. I just need to think about all this."

Sophie nodded, although looking not at all convinced that she would ever see her parents again.

The rest of that afternoon was spent making several large lasagnas in Uncle Maynard's kitchen. Making food is often a good thing to do when life looks very difficult, and Uncle Maynard was an excellent cook.

"It's always good to have lots of frozen lasagnas when disaster strikes!" he said. "That way, you'll always be able to put together a quick hot meal when you're in a hurry. That's one thing I've learned over the years."

William also played the violin for Sophie and Uncle Maynard, although he was frequently interrupted by his uncle, who coached him on various technical aspects of his instrument. William imagined that he ought to be treated a bit more gently, seeing what he had gone through that day. But the violin was a very serious matter for Uncle Maynard, and, as he often said, "A young musician must understand all his mistakes if he intends to get better."

At any rate, after an afternoon and evening of cooking and violin playing, Uncle Maynard turned the television back on–it was eight o'clock–and the three gathered around to hear the mayor's announcement.

The patriotic collage and the patriotic music played for some time. Finally, at ten past eight, the television went blank. And then there was a shot of a set of curtains and a podium. This scene played for a few minutes. After this, the mayor walked on-screen and stood behind the podium. He was a tall man, and his stomach and chest were also fairly large–

almost what you would call fat, but not quite. He had a strong, square chin. His hair was graying and slightly wavy. And he had black, steady eyes. He was also clean shaven, although he had the kind of face that would look very good with a large bristly moustache. The fact was that he was very intimidating, and very authoritative, and on this particular night, he looked very serious.

After arriving at the podium, the mayor paused for a few moments before the camera. Then he cleared his throat and began speaking. "Citizens of Willoughby," he said. "I thank you for joining me during such troubled times. These have been hard days for everyone. We have all lost a great deal. And we are all uncertain about what hardships await us. But I am here tonight to say that times are changing.

The national government is in chaos. But your local leaders are squarely in charge. And I have a historic announcement to make. I am announcing tonight that I have formed a new peace agreement with the aliens."

"My goodness!" Uncle Maynard said. "I can't imagine this is a very good development."

"Citizens," the mayor said, "just today, using our brilliant translators from the University of Willoughby, I have communicated with the alien leaders, and I am here to tell you that this race of beings is gravely misunderstood." This was a fairly strange assertion, seeing that eating people was hardly a difficult thing to understand. But the mayor explained the matter like this: "They thought we were something like cows or chickens, which we human beings eat all the time. Now that they understand that we are not like cows and chickens, they will not be eating us. So long as we stay out of their way, help them when our help is asked for, and promise not to leave the city limits of Willoughby.

"The aliens are planning on leaving soon," he continued. "This is good. We will all be able to get back to our regular way of life. But the aliens need to find a cure for the disease that they've been suffering from."

The mayor took a deep breath and looked sad and pained. "And I think we can all agree that they have suffered a great deal from this terrible disease. A great deal."

Suddenly, patriotic music began playing again, while the mayor stared directly into the camera. He had a firm, determined look on his face, although to the observers in Uncle Maynard's kitchen, it also seemed to be a look of insanity.

"And so," the mayor said, "I would like to conclude by welcoming everyone into a new era of cooperation!" At this point, the camera frame began to change. It pulled back, and the screen started to show more of what was happening on either side of the mayor. And there, to the mayor's right, was another man, standing between two enormous and extremely hideous aliens. The other man was tall and handsome and smiling as though a wonderful day had finally arrived. The aliens, however, looked fairly upset by the whole situation, snarling and gnashing their teeth as they were. Of course, no one had ever seen an alien who wasn't biting someone's arm off, or chasing a lady down the street, or firing some kind of laser bomb into someone's house. So, judged from that perspective, these aliens seemed to be relatively peaceful. Still, even the mayor was not quite sure how he ought to behave, and as he walked over to shake the aliens' strange alien hands, he looked very uneasy.

And it was equally mystifying to William and Sophie and Uncle Maynard. Each of them stared at the television with stunned looks on their faces.

But Sophie's face was the most stunned of all. William looked at his two companions as the speech came to an end, and noticed Sophie looking like she was desperately trying to process some terrible piece of information.

"This is good news, Sophie," William said, trying to reassure her, although he didn't really believe what he said.

Sophie hesitated. Finally, though, she managed to speak. "That man!" she said.

"The mayor?" William replied.

"No, the man between the aliens."

Now Uncle Maynard was looking down at her as well. "Yes?"

"That's the man who was with the aliens when they took my parents!"

At this, Uncle Maynard raised his eyebrows. "Remarkable," he said. "Very remarkable."

And then, after a pause, he said, "Well I happen to know the mayor very well. So perhaps we can go find him, and this man he hangs around with, and they can tell us just where your parents are."

8

After some discussion, our three heroes conceived a small plan. They would pay a visit to their friend the mayor to demand that he help Sophie find her parents. But it was now late in the evening, and all of them agreed that it was best to wait until the next day. Despite the mayor's claim that the aliens wanted peace, our friends concluded that the aliens would likely still eat them if they got the chance. Running around in the dark seemed not to be a very good idea.

So instead, the three of them spent time in the kitchen, playing the violin, eating dinner (a very large lasagna), and talking about what they thought would happen next in the world.

William was also trying to get used to the idea that his stepparents were gone. "It's just very strange, finding someone's feet like that," he said over and over.

And it *was* strange. And very disturbing. But he also found that he felt a kind of lightness and freedom that he had never quite felt before–or at least not since his real parents had been alive.

"But I just wonder what will happen next," he said.

"Well, you can always stay with me," Uncle Maynard replied as he tightened the horsehair on his violin bow. "Of course, who knows what will happen with these aliens? We might just get eaten ourselves."

Uncle Maynard laughed as he said this, but William did not find this idea very funny. Still, he was happy with the notion that he might now live with his uncle.

Over the years, Uncle Maynard had been a very great friend to William. After William's parents died and his brother ran away, he was basically alone in

the world, except for his stepparents, who (obviously) didn't like him very much. In fact, their presence made William feel even more alone, even though they were always walking around the house, yelling at him and interfering with his violin playing.

Now, it would not be inappropriate to wonder why William didn't leave his stepparents and go to live with his uncle. In many ways, this would have been the best arrangement for everybody. But (as is often the case in this sort of situation) money was involved, namely an allowance that William received from his parents' estate. The money was not a huge amount, but it was enough to make it worthwhile for his stepparents to retain legal guardianship over him, seeing that they were greedy people and this legal understanding allowed them to decide how the money was spent.

At any rate, during the terrible time following his father's death, William depended on his uncle a great deal. William spent whatever time he could at Uncle Maynard's house, studying violin, drinking tea, watching television (when Uncle Maynard could tolerate it), and eating the peculiar dinners that

Uncle Maynard liked to prepare. And as that particular night wore on, and the violin playing and the lasagna eating had concluded, and as William eventually found himself getting ready for bed, he continued thinking very deeply about all these things. As he turned down his covers and pulled back his sheets, he considered how kind Uncle Maynard had been to him for his whole life. And after shutting off the light (it was a very old lamp, on an ancient bedside table, in a mostly empty bedroom, in a far corner of the third floor of the mansion), William couldn't help but think about the details of an extremely bad day at school he had had about a year and a half earlier, not long after his brother had run away to Great Harbor–a day in which his uncle had helped him out quite a bit.

At the very strict school that William's stepparents sent him to, teachers frequently punished students by taunting them, pushing them, slapping them, and even beating them with their shoes. And William always seemed to be getting the worst of it, although it was true that he was usually a bit dreamy. One day, a particular teacher decided that William was spending far too much time looking out the window. He walked around the classroom as he lectured about rainfall, weather patterns, and continental geography. And while William was happily staring out the window at a small cluster of swallows darting through the trees, the teacher came up behind him and slapped him (very hard) on the back of his head. Again, such punishment was not unusual at William's school. And William found that he was often being slapped. The thing was that this time, it seemed to hurt far more than usual. And it was extremely unexpected. If you're watching a cluster of swallows darting through trees and suddenly someone slaps you in the back of the head, it can be quite alarming.

Now, William normally took this kind of abuse silently. What was there for him to do? And it was certainly not in William's nature to be violent. He was, in fact, what most people would consider to be extremely gentle. But on this particular day, he was in a bad mood. His stepparents had woken him up at four in the morning to pull weeds from the vegetable garden. Because of this, William was very tired and feeling very abused. And this teacher, whose name happened to be Mr. Hesselwhite, had always been extremely mean to him. So William rubbed his head, looked back at his teacher, and then, in an act of astonishing bravado, stood up and punched him right in the stomach.

Needless to say, this was not a good idea. It made William feel good at the time. That was true. But in the long run, it really was not a good idea. After being slapped some more, William was dragged to the headmaster's office (Mr. Hesselwhite, by the way, was a very large man) and William's stepparents were called in. And when they arrived, there was another round of slapping and yelling, during which William was called "shameful beast," "ungrateful pig," "little monster," and numerous other things that no young boy ever ought to hear. William thought about punching everyone in the stomach again. They deserved it, as far as he was concerned. (And what fair-minded person would disagree with him?) But people can't do everything they want, and William well knew that if he started throwing punches again, he'd never make it home alive. So he kept his seat, bit his tongue, and took the slapping and name-calling without uttering another word. It was a terrible moment, and as William drove home with his step-parents nearly half an hour later, they continued to call him names and to tell him just how much worse it was going to get for him–extra chores, earlier bedtime, and absolutely no violin playing.

The next day, however, (a Saturday), William decided to sneak away for a few hours–he could hardly get in more trouble. He jumped on a city bus and headed to his uncle's house. Soon he found himself sitting in Uncle Maynard's enormous kitchen, crying bitterly and telling his uncle the entire story.

The whole time Uncle Maynard just shook his head and said, "Terrible! Just terrible!"

Normally, Uncle Maynard did not like to interfere with William's home life. He was never happy about the suffering that William had to endure. But Uncle Maynard also knew that he really had no authority over William's stepparents, and that his interference would only make things worse. Also, there was the risk that William would be prevented from ever seeing him. This was often threatened. On this occasion, though, William's treatment struck him as very unfair, especially because it all started with watching a cluster of swallows, a sort of bird that Uncle Maynard had always loved.

"Of course, you should never punch your teachers in the stomach," Uncle Maynard said. "That's never the best course of action. But I understand why you did it." And then, after thinking a bit more, Uncle Maynard added, "I think that I can help you out a bit on this though."

It was true, Uncle Maynard was a bit of a hermit. But he was also a world-famous musician. And he had a long history of hobnobbing with Willoughby's social elites. He knew many important people (like the mayor, for instance). Many people respected him. And others were even slightly afraid of him. At any rate, after William finished his story and got ready to leave, Uncle Maynard said again that he might be able to help him out. "But just this once," he said. "To straighten things out a bit. But William, I advise you not to punch anyone else in the stomach. One day you might punch the wrong person, and you'll get more than a few slaps."

William nodded. He really did agree with this,

although he wondered just how much more slapping he could take at home and at school.

William went home, and for the next several days he skulked around the house and around school, doing his extra chores and listening politely as Mr. Hesselwhite continued to call him "monster" and "beast." And then one day something extraordinary happened. William was pulled into the hall, just before classes began, and Mr. Hesselwhite (looking very nervous and very angry) said that perhaps the two of them ought to learn to be friends.

"Perhaps I've been too hard on you," he said. "Perhaps it's best if you and I try to get along a bit better. Maybe we should try to be friends. And I'd like to say that I'm very sorry for slapping you so frequently." As Mr. Hesselwhite said this, his teeth were clenched as though the idea of anything like friendship between the two was the very worst thing that he could imagine.

"Okay," William replied, unsure of what else to say and entirely baffled by this apology.

William learned the origins of Mr. Hesselwhite's bizarre behavior later that afternoon, although it was not too far from what he expected. He was at his uncle's house eating crackers and salted fish and telling the story of Mr. Hesselwhite's apology, when he said, "But I think you probably know all about this."

Uncle Maynard paused for a moment, and then said, "Well, I have a close friend who happens to be on the board of directors of your school." Uncle Maynard now looked sideways at William for a moment, and then said, "Between you and me, Mr. Hesselwhite is in a bit of trouble himself. Apparently, there's been some school money missing. And there's some question as to whether Mr. Hesselwhite might be involved. He's not in very good standing with the board of directors at the moment. The headmaster adores him. But your headmaster is also a very nasty man. At any rate, Mr. Hesselwhite is in some trouble, and my friend on the board has been reviewing his case, and might possibly have had a word with him about you. Although it doesn't sound like Mr. Hesselwhite's apology was very sincere."

"It wasn't," William said. "But it was good enough. I just don't want him to slap the back of my head anymore."

"And that seems like a very reasonable thing to

ask for," Uncle Maynard said. "It's not like you're demanding anything special."

It is worth noting that on the day that the aliens arrived in Willoughby, Mr. Hesselwhite was one of the first people to be eaten. Again, William was never happy when anyone got eaten. All the same, as William thought about this event (lying in bed on the night that he arrived at Uncle Maynard's), he decided that the aliens seemed to have a taste for many of the bad people in his life. But then William thought about all the other people who had been eaten–all the people who didn't deserve anything but happiness but who were eaten anyway–and William once again realized that the world was indeed facing a terrible calamity, and that there was no rhyme or reason whatsoever as to why one person was attacked while another was spared. It made things seem very grim. But he was now at his uncle's house, and safe for the moment, and he imagined that if anyone could protect him, and help Sophie find her parents, it was definitely his uncle. And thinking this, William finally fell asleep.

9

The next morning, William awoke to the smell of bacon and the clanging of pots and pans. His room was far from the kitchen, but the ventilation system in Uncle Maynard's house was not very modern, and it carried sounds and smells throughout the house. It reminded him of long ago, when his real parents were still alive, and he awoke every morning to happy, amused activity. His stepparents slept late, never cooked anything, and they certainly never made breakfast for him. Usually the morning began with them complaining about his violin playing or ridiculing him for being such a bad student. As William lay on his back in bed that morning, he thought about how much better it was to wake up to a bacony smell and the sounds of Uncle Maynard dashing around.

When William finally arrived in the kitchen (still extremely tired) he found that Sophie, too, was already awake, and his uncle was giving her instructions on how to chop vegetables for their omelets.

"Just like this," he said, chopping a fistful of green onions like a sort of wild animal, banging the knife against the cutting board at an incredible rate of speed.

Sophie gave Uncle Maynard a puzzled look, paused for a second, and then said, "I think I'd just prefer to do it slowly, thank you very much."

"Suit yourself," Uncle Maynard said, frowning and handing the knife back to her. "But you'll take all morning at the rate you're going."

Then Uncle Maynard turned around and saw William standing in the doorway. "William!" he said, "I thought you might have been eaten by creatures from outer space. But I see now that you've just been sleeping late."

It was only seven thirty and William hardly felt that this was late. But before he could respond, Uncle Maynard quickly said, "Are you alert enough to beat the eggs?"

"I guess so," William replied, and in the next instant he was standing at a counter beating a bowlful of eggs with a whisk.

Preparations took another fifteen minutes, and when they were finally done cooking, the three sat down to a small feast of bacon, eggs, oatmeal, baked beans, sardines, toast, butter, jam, and coffee.

"We need to eat a big breakfast," Uncle Maynard said. "I expect that today will be quite eventful. I just hope that the mayor will agree to see us." (Incidentally, the mayor's name was Preston Walters, which is how Uncle Maynard will occasionally refer to him from this point forward.)

"Preston Walters is just like you," Uncle Maynard continued, looking at William. "Not very alert in the morning. But I think we'll be able to get some answers out of him. I've known him for long enough that he'll be straight with us." Uncle Maynard tightened the scarf that still hung around his neck and then scooped a big bite of egg into his mouth. "Preston Walters, the mayor!" he continued, his mouth now full of food. "It's one of the most ridiculous things I've ever seen in my entire life. It's been twenty years since he was elected, but I'll never get over it. Preston Walters!"

Uncle Maynard looked up and began inspecting the various things on the table. Finally, he frowned and said, "I wish we had fresh fruit. How things have changed in so short a time!"

It occurred to William that his uncle was extremely animated and that maybe this was how he always was in the morning–the fact was that they hadn't shared too many breakfasts. William, however, wasn't ever very quick in the morning (as his uncle had already pointed out), and after about a minute of thinking over his uncle's energetic behavior, his mind grew tired, and he began to focus on the matter at hand: his omelet.

"This is delicious," he finally said, after taking a few bites.

"It is indeed," Uncle Maynard quickly replied.

Breakfast concluded in silence, our three friends growing full and slightly tired because of it. Eventually Uncle Maynard got up and turned on the kettle, and then said, "Perhaps we should see if there's any news on." He walked to the television, switched it on, and then yelled, "Television in the morning! It's unbearable!" Then he started shifting through the channels.

It is worth noting that about this time in the

course of the First Invasion, a strange channel started appearing on televisions around Willoughby. It was faint at first. Just a lot of black and white dots. But as days passed (after aliens began to get sicker, and before William's stepparents were eaten), the channel became stronger and stronger. Its origins were the Northern Empire, and its message was clear: aliens had been losing ground in the north, and humans had established a free colony there; people were encouraged to flee there from their enslaved cities. And it was on this channel that Uncle Maynard suddenly halted.

"The aliens must not win," an announcer said. The announcer sat in a small studio and was surrounded by people rushing around with folders and handfuls of computer printouts. "You must do all you can to escape to the north." Then the screen suddenly started fading out, and before long, the TV was just a staticky gray blur.

"The Northern Empire!" Uncle Maynard said. "I can't say I much want to go there. But given how things are moving in Willoughby, that just may be where we end up."

"It sounds better than down here," Sophie said.

William looked over at his violin and wondered if he really cared where they went, so long as he was with his uncle and he had his violin. And then he suddenly and unexpectedly thought about his brother for a moment and wondered if his brother was even still alive. But this thought was so painful that in the next instant, William found himself standing on the other side of the room, playing a sad folk song on his violin as he watched his uncle and Sophie begin to clear the breakfast table.

10

As you might imagine, getting ready for the trip to City Hall was quite a production. Uncle Maynard had a large, trucklike car (quite popular at the time), which he drove with great recklessness. He was really little better at driving than William, and all his neighbors would stand far from the road when they saw him careening by. Fortunately, he rarely drove, preferring to ride his bicycle to most places around the city of Willoughby. And on a bicycle, he was quite safe and reliable.

Since Uncle Maynard's car was large and sturdy, it was ideal for braving hoards of aliens who might try to eat them. Obviously, if the aliens wanted, it would not be hard for them to stop the car and quickly empty it out and eat the contents. But, again, these aliens were extremely lazy and were rarely tempted by a large trucklike car flying down the street at high speeds, especially when there were so many other easy targets just sitting around in their living rooms doing nothing. Of course, with the mayor's announcement of the new peace, it seemed that such protection shouldn't be necessary. But none of our three heroes believed that this peace could be real, given what they'd seen.

In addition to the sturdy car, Uncle Maynard also had quite a collection of weapons, some of which had once belonged to aliens and which he had bought on the underground market–a hard thing to do; they were rare and very expensive.

"You can't have enough of these!" Uncle Maynard said, pointing to a now unlocked and wide-open closetful of alien ray guns just off the kitchen.

"Um, what were you planning to do with these?" Sophie said, staring in disbelief.

"I was planning on keeping myself alive," Uncle Maynard said. He took one from the closet, held it in his hands, and (all of a sudden and quite accidentally) shot a crashing electric beam into a large stuffed chair that sat in the far corner of the room. The chair immediately dissolved into dust.

The three stared at the chair with a look of horror.

"Sorry about that," Uncle Maynard said, laughing nervously. "I suppose we ought to be careful with these."

Sophie looked at William in panic.

"We'll be careful," William promised.

After putting on warm clothes and then packing up three alien guns, several sandwiches, and a tin of cookies, the three walked out the back door on their

way to Uncle Maynard's car. Uncle Maynard carefully locked up the many locks on his back door and set the alarm. Then they all clambered aboard Uncle Maynard's boxy vehicle, and in seconds, they were charging wildly down the streets of Willoughby.

11

The drive to City Hall was not far. But Uncle Maynard took several back streets, to avoid places where aliens were known to hang around. "I don't think we should take any chances with this new 'peace' of the mayor's," he said as they weaved down an alleyway a few blocks from his house.

"I think that's a good idea," William replied, although it now occurred to him that he might very well die in a car crash, given how his uncle was driving. He looked over just as his uncle had taken both hands off the steering wheel to adjust his scarf. William almost said something, but Sophie beat him to it.

"He's almost as good a driver as you, William," she said with a very deliberate sarcastic tone.

"Is that an insult?" Uncle Maynard quickly said. "I won't have my driving insulted."

"It's just that I'd prefer not to die in your car, thank you," Sophie replied.

"No one's going to die with me around!" Uncle Maynard said, hoisting both his fists in the air and letting go of the wheel again.

"You make me feel very safe," Sophie said.

"Is that sarcasm? Another insult?" Uncle Maynard snapped.

At any rate, the trip took about ten minutes, and when they arrived, City Hall looked rather busy. People were heading in and out at a very rapid pace. There didn't appear to be any aliens around, although there were several of their aircraft at rest near the back of the building. They were monstrous-looking machines with strange arms and lights and windows popping out on all sides. They were beetle black and seemed to be almost alive, almost like some kind of giant horrible insects had arrived and parked themselves outside of City Hall. It was a fairly sickening sight, and Uncle Maynard, William, and Sophie took in the scene for nearly a minute before Uncle Maynard finally sighed, unbuckled his seat belt, and then said, "All right. Let's go."

William quickly unbuckled his seat belt–Sophie did the same–and soon they were following Uncle Maynard across the street and toward City Hall.

It was generally believed that City Hall was one of the nicest buildings in Willoughby. It was an enormous stone building with large gray columns surrounding it and several gigantic bronze doors at the

entrance. It was built by the mayor shortly after he was elected, some twenty years earlier, and he had worked there ever since. The mayor's personal offices were also supposed to be beautiful. In fact, there had been complaining when they were built. Critics asked if this was really the best use of the people's money. But the mayor was a shrewd businessman and a big-time deal maker, and, as he often pointed out, he brought enough business into

Willoughby to make up for whatever he spent on his beautiful offices.

Interestingly, Uncle Maynard had played a minor role in getting the mayor elected. Seeing that Uncle Maynard was something of a world-class musical celebrity, and a very rich man, he was a good ally to have around Willoughby. Uncle Maynard was against doing too much to help Mr. Preston Walters, but the soon-to-be mayor promised to double the city's musical education budget if he was elected. And it was also true that Uncle Maynard was close friends with Preston Walters's father. Preston Senior was a scientist and had made an absolutely colossal fortune inventing a type of extra-strong plastic bag. He had even given Uncle Maynard money when he was a young composer. So Uncle Maynard felt some kind of obligation to the family. He showed up at a few campaign parties, shook a few hands, played an occasional mazurka on the violin, and generally told people that Preston Walters was a highly unique individual, which, after all, was entirely true. Uncle Maynard did wonder if he was doing the right thing. But he had also imagined that it all wasn't very important in the end.

"He can't possibly last for too long," he told friends. "Just long enough to increase the musical education budget."

Sadly, however, he lasted a very long time. And he didn't do very much in the end to improve musical education. Nevertheless, in the shadow of an alien-led planetary catastrophe, it was not such a bad thing to have the mayor owe you a favor.

When the three arrived in the broad lobby of City Hall, they were quickly greeted by several large security guards. Everyone was being stopped. It was nothing personal. But William wasn't entirely happy about being inspected and probed by large people wearing guns. It was good that their own guns were still in the car, because (as is well known) carrying around a large alien firearm tends to arouse people's suspicions.

"Getting shoved around like this is just like being at our school," William said as they were finally released from the rough inspection.

"I think this is a little worse," Sophie said.

"I don't think so," William replied. "Nothing is worse than school."

Sophie looked quizzically at William for a moment and seemed as though she was about to say something in response, but she was soon distracted. She looked about her, as did William, and stared up at the enormous domed ceiling and wide marble arches. William was now feeling somewhat intimidated, and from Sophie's wide-eyed gaze, it seemed that she was now feeling the same way as well. It was a puzzling feeling, but in another instant, William returned to practical matters as he and Sophie and Uncle Maynard stepped up to a large marble desk where five people in uniform were directing people to various places in the building.

"Can I help you?" a tall, thin woman asked. Uncle Maynard opened his mouth to reply but suddenly let forth a kind of strange coughing fit. It lasted for nearly ninety seconds, during which time the tall woman turned her head and rolled her eyes.

As Uncle Maynard's coughing slowed, he put his hand over his heart, looked at William, and said, "I'm in no condition for this. My heart is beating a mile a minute, and is definitely off rhythm."

William didn't quite know what to say. He'd

heard this a million times before, but it always worried him. Just as he was about to suggest that they sit down for a moment, though, the woman behind the counter again snapped, "Can I help you?"

Uncle Maynard put his hand on the counter and said, "We'd like to see the mayor."

The woman blinked several times, as though this was the most ridiculous request she had ever heard. "I'm afraid the mayor isn't seeing anyone at the moment," she finally said.

"Yes, well, I happen to be an old friend of his," Uncle Maynard replied, still holding on to the counter. "I think if you asked him, you'd find that he'd want to see me."

"I think he wouldn't," the woman said, glaring at Uncle Maynard's scruffy appearance.

"I think he would."

"He's extremely busy," the woman replied. "I'm afraid, Mr. . . . Mr. . . . I'm sorry, what's your name?"

"Bright. Maynard Bright."

Suddenly the woman's eyebrows raised. "The composer?" she said.

"Yes, the composer." Uncle Maynard loosened his scarf and wiped his brow. "The world-famous, much-celebrated, ballyhooed composer." Uncle Maynard was now speaking in a slightly sarcastic tone–something that seemed to amuse Sophie a great deal.

"I . . . I just love your work," the woman behind the desk said. "It's such an honor to meet you." She paused, then said, "Let me see if I can get ahold of the mayor's secretary."

"Thank you," Uncle Maynard replied. Then, still holding his hand to his chest, he looked at William and Sophie and said, "I think I need to sit down for a moment. I just tend to get a bit excited in this kind of situation. Imagine asking Preston Walters for a favor! How things have changed! Wait here and let me know what happens." Uncle Maynard then walked slowly to a bench at the side of the lobby.

The woman began dialing and apparently had to call several numbers before she could get any help. Finally, someone appeared to answer her phone call. The woman turned around, whispered a few things into the phone, listened for a second, and then hung up.

"The mayor will be notified that you are here," she said, turning back toward William and Sophie. "If he has time to see you, his secretary will let you know. Maybe it's best if you wait over there with Mr. Bright."

William and Sophie looked over at Uncle Maynard, who had unbuttoned his thick wool cardigan and the top buttons of his shirt. He looked like he was breathing more easily now. They headed over to him to take a seat on the bench, but by the time they arrived, the telephone rang, and the woman behind the counter was quickly calling for them.

"Excuse me," she said. "Mr. Bright. The mayor is about to leave the building, but he'll see you for just a minute right now." Then she pointed toward another door and said, "Go to security. They'll show you the way."

"Thank you," Uncle Maynard said, standing up again. He still appeared tired but had a more determined look on his face.

The security man at the door was a little bigger and more athletic than the ones at the main entrance. He wore a black suit rather than a uniform and had a narrow mustache and short, pointed sideburns. He checked them for weapons again, running his hands up and down their clothing. Then he barked something in code into his walkie-talkie, waved the three in through the door, and said, "Go to the end of the hallway just through this door, and then make a left. You can only see him for a minute. He has to leave the building. You can speak to him as he walks down the hall."

Suddenly Uncle Maynard looked extremely flustered. "I can only talk to him as he walks down the hall?" he finally said.

"I'm sorry," the man replied. "That's all the time he has." All at once, the man looked very grave. "Given the circumstances, I think you should be grateful that he'll see you at all."

"Grateful!" Uncle Maynard shouted, now buttoning the buttons of his cardigan back up and tightening his scarf. "Grateful, indeed! I don't think so. Not to see Preston Walters."

William watched his uncle as he turned and headed down the hall. "Come on William and Sophie," he said. "We'll have to make do with what we have."

William and Sophie paused for a moment and then turned and followed Uncle Maynard toward the mayor.

12

As often happened in moments of great stress, William suddenly found himself thinking about his parents and his brother. As he walked down the halls behind his uncle, following the clipped directions of the various security guards, he considered all that had happened to him over the years and wondered if losing people he loved (and people he decidedly did not love) was just the natural state of things in the world.

City Hall was buzzing with activity as William considered this. Office workers were rushing by, all chattering about the mayor's speech and the "new peace." Some thought it was extremely promising. Others thought that the situation was entirely hopeless. But as William heard all this, he began to wonder if aliens being on Earth really mattered one way or another. He thought about the day that his father died–semiconscious, on a hospital bed, with tubes running in and out of his body–and he decided that the world could be a very terrible place even without aliens. And he thought about that night, going home with his stepmother, who had never liked him at all and was as unhappy about being alone with him as he was with her. His stepmother cried all through that night. She was a terrible person, and she would soon prove to be more terrible than even William could imagine, and yet she was also so sad. It was strange to William–this capacity for enormous sorrow in even the most heartless of people–and it was strange that William was able to feel so much sympathy for her that night.

William looked over at Sophie and thought about how she must be feeling, given the situation her parents were in. As they followed one hall after another, she kept looking more and more anxious, and William felt that he ought to say something to her, something to comfort her. But he couldn't quite find the right words. Everything just seemed so confusing. What William most wanted at that moment was to be back at his uncle's house, eating lasagna, playing his violin, and watching Sophie chop vegetables in her slow and deliberate manner.

Suddenly William was lifted from his thoughts. As they turned another corner, Uncle Maynard came to a swift halt. William looked down the hall, and before them was a pack of men in black suits with guns, ushering the mayor down the hall. The men were moving rapidly and in silence. But then, all at once, the silence broke.

"Hello, Maynard!" the mayor said in a loud and serious voice. Uncle Maynard stepped forward as the security guards parted. The two men shook hands as the mayor looked grimly into Uncle Maynard's eyes. They were now all standing near a door labeled MAYOR'S OFFICE.

"These are terrible times," the mayor said. "Terrible times. But I think I've found a way through it all. With courage and determination, the citizens of Willoughby can make it through."

William watched Sophie roll her eyes. And Uncle Maynard, too, looked like he wanted to make some expression of disgust, like he was about to start screaming about how ridiculous it was that this man was in charge of anything. But he managed to keep quiet. He merely nodded, looked very serious, and said, "Yes. Courage and determination. The citizens of Willoughby will surely be forever grateful to you."

Then the mayor said, "My secretary told me that you needed something?" The men in black suits had carefully moved into a kind of circle around them all.

Uncle Maynard reached to his side and put his hand on Sophie's shoulder. "I'm looking for this girl's parents," he replied. "Doctor and Doctor Astronovitch. And a man. He was on the television last night. Standing behind you. The Doctors Astronovitch were taken from their house yesterday by the aliens. The man we're looking for was with them."

The mayor looked puzzled for a moment, then said, "Who are Doctor and Doctor Astronovitch? I'm afraid I've never heard of them."

"Medical researchers. From the university."

The mayor scratched his chin. "I'm sorry to say I don't know anything about them. It all sounds very unusual though. I don't know that I've heard of anyone being taken by aliens like that before. Eaten maybe. But never *taken*."

"Well they were!" Sophie said, speaking up unexpectedly. "Who was the man on television with you last night?"

The mayor smiled slightly and paused. Then he stepped forward, closer to Uncle Maynard, and said in a much lower voice, "These are very difficult times, Maynard. But if we all remain calm, things will work themselves out. I've talked to these aliens. They won't hurt us if we stay calm. For now, I think you should just head home and relax."

The mayor then stepped back a bit, took a deep breath, and opened the door to his office. He was now smiling slightly and nodding. "It's been so nice to see you. Please get in touch if there's anything else that you need."

The mayor entered the office, followed by his bodyguards, and the door was shut behind them. William wondered what would be next, and half expected his uncle to begin screaming. But as William looked up at his uncle, he noticed that he was now looking away from the mayor's office and down the hall.

William turned to see what Uncle Maynard was

looking at, and there, at the end of the hall, standing with two bodyguards, was the man they had seen on TV, the man Sophie had seen take away her parents.

"That's the man!" William quickly said.

"I see, William. I see."

Now Sophie looked down the hall as well. But just as she did, the man disappeared behind a door.

13

It was a strange moment: there was the man they were looking for, but it wasn't clear what they should do. William thought that they should try to follow him. But Uncle Maynard seemed to have other plans. In the next instant, he was once again banging on the door to the mayor's office.

In a few seconds the door swung open, and a large bodyguard appeared. "Yes?" he said.

"I need to see the mayor again!" Uncle Maynard yelled.

"The mayor has left the building," the bodyguard replied.

"What?" Uncle Maynard said.

"He's left the building. He has a back exit. For security."

"Well, you've got to get him for us."

"I don't even know who you are."

"I'm a very old friend of the mayor's."

"How do I know that? Anyway, it's too late now."

The bodyguard leaned back and pointed at a large picture window at the back of the mayor's office.

Uncle Maynard, William, and Sophie all stretched their necks to see through the window. Outside, on the lawn, was a large helicopter, and the mayor was walking toward it. Uncle Maynard moved forward, perhaps thinking that he might be able to run out and catch him. But the bodyguard's hand came up.

"I can't let you come through," he said.

Uncle Maynard started to reply, but the mayor was now walking up the small metal steps to the helicopter.

"You must let me speak to him!" he said in another instant.

"It's too late. I'd be happy to give him a message though."

The mayor was now in the helicopter, and the door slowly started to close. The helicopter was enormous, and William noticed that it seemed to be filled with strange tubes and stands and boxes marked "Willoughby University." It was a perplexing sight, the mayor sandwiching himself in among all those boxes and all that equipment. But William's view quickly changed. The helicopter began to lift off the ground.

William looked up at Uncle Maynard, who suddenly pulled away from the bodyguard and darted down the hall.

"Follow me!" he said to the two young people. They quickly started running and were soon close on Uncle Maynard's heels.

In about two seconds, they arrived at the door that the other man had just entered, and Uncle Maynard immediately began to knock. William watched as he rapped his knuckles against the large oak door, and noticed that his uncle had become very pale and sweaty. Still, he looked determined to keep going.

In another second the door opened. Again, it was another bodyguard.

"Yes?" the man said.

But none of our three heroes could manage a response. They were too stunned by what they saw inside the large office. The man from the television was nowhere in sight. But standing about five feet behind the bodyguard were two aliens, holding huge, cannonlike guns, swaying slightly in their robotic leggings, and hissing and rattling in their hideous alien language.

William watched as Uncle Maynard tried to think of what to say. But in the next second, Sophie stepped forward and shouted, "Where's the man that just came in here?"

"I'm afraid that I don't know who you're talking about, sweetheart," the bodyguard replied in a very slimy tone.

"The man who just came in here!" Sophie yelled, now even more angry. For a moment, she looked as though she might try to push her way past the guard. But just then, the two aliens stepped toward the door and stared directly at her with their grotesque beady eyes.

"You have to leave," the bodyguard said quickly, now sounding a little nervous. Then one of the aliens stepped even closer, looking as hostile as this type of alien can look. His teeth were showing, his nose holes were gaping open and filled with some kind of slime, a hand was holding the trigger of his gun, and his tentacles were waving and vibrating above him. At that moment, William imagined that he would soon be just a pair of bodiless feet, lying on the floor of City Hall. But the alien simply stepped forward with its strange robotic leggings, grabbed hold of the door, and slammed it shut.

Sophie put up her hand to start knocking again, apparently unafraid of anything at this point. But Uncle Maynard quickly grabbed her hand and held it back.

"Let's consider this a bit," he said. "I don't think we're going to get very far here."

Uncle Maynard pulled his scarf tighter, coughed some, and then closed his eyes to think. He was silent for several moments, when unexpectedly, from behind another door, a woman appeared. "May I talk to you for a second, please?" she whispered.

"Of course," Uncle Maynard replied, opening his eyes.

"Come over here," she said, leading them to a little corner at the other side of the hall. When they all stepped over, she said, "I understand you're looking for the Astronovitches?"

"Yes," Sophie quickly answered.

"I'm almost positive they're at the mayor's mansion on Starling Lake. The man in there is Caldwell Jones. He's one of the mayor's deputies. I know that he's been helping to capture people who might be useful to the aliens. And he's taken them to Starling Lake."

The woman paused for a moment, and then looked down at Sophie. "They're your parents, right?"

"Yes," Sophie replied.

"I'm sure they're all right. I think that the aliens need them. They're doctors, correct?"

"Yes," Sophie said again.

"I'm sure they're alive. The aliens need their help with this disease they're suffering from. I'm sure your parents are still alive," the woman said again.

And then, "The aliens killed my husband. This peace will never last. They're horrible creatures. The mayor must know that. He thinks this is going to get him something–this pact he's arranged."

Again the woman paused.

"Mayor Walters and Caldwell Jones won't be back for a while," she resumed. "And everything is under wraps. They're not saying anything. But I do know that the mayor and Mr. Jones are now also going to be spending all their time at the Starling Lake mansion. They're running everything from there. Plenty of fresh water and food. No concerned citizens of Willoughby asking difficult questions. They have a helicopter pad. They have a small television studio set up where they can broadcast messages. And it's where they're meeting with the aliens. More importantly, I've heard that they have some kind of lab set up there. The mayor's father built it years ago. It was built inside a renovated barn. Very state of the art. It was where he did his scientific experiments and invented his plastics. They're shipping all kinds of equipment up there. Medical equipment. I think your parents are there. I'm pretty sure they're there.

Still, so many people are missing." She paused. "And so many have been killed. But I'm almost positive they're there."

William looked over at Uncle Maynard, expecting some kind of reply, but he had started looking very sick and had loosened his scarf again so that he could breathe more easily. William wondered if he had even heard what this woman had told them.

"This has been very helpful," William finally said.

The woman looked at William and said, "Come find me again if you need anything. Anything at all." Then she turned and walked quickly down the hall.

William looked up at Uncle Maynard, who looked down and said softly, "I really think I should get home. I need to take my medicine. I know I'm quite a complainer, William and Sophie. But I really am not well."

"Whatever you need, Uncle Maynard," William said. He looked over at Sophie, who seemed lost in thought.

Uncle Maynard looked at Sophie as well and quickly said, "We'll go to Starling Lake, Sophie. We'll get your parents out of there. But let's go home now to regroup. I need to take my medicine."

Uncle Maynard looked slightly confused for a second, and then walked off to his right. "Follow me," he said, and he headed toward a door marked EXIT. It wasn't the way they had come in, but it seemed as good a way out as any.

"I need air," Uncle Maynard said as he pushed open the heavy metal door. Soon William, Sophie, and Uncle Maynard found themselves on a side street behind the City Hall building. They turned left and headed back to the car. But as they were walking, Sophie suddenly came to an abrupt halt. She turned her head away and pointed to the ground. There, in a small pile, lay several pairs of glistening, bloody feet.

"Those people have just been eaten," Uncle Maynard said, the color still drained from his cheeks. "So much for the peace. I suggest we get to the car."

It was only about twenty feet to the main street, and they made it there in a few seconds. William quickly spotted Uncle Maynard's car, and in just another instant, they were piling in, ready to return home to plan their next move.

14

Starling Lake was nearly two hours away from Willoughby. It was where Willoughby's richest and most celebrated citizens had summer homes, and the mayor was known to have an enormous fortresslike mansion there, with lots of land and several buildings. Uncle Maynard also had a place in that area, although it was only a cottage by a small apple orchard, about fifteen miles away from the lake.

"It's the only place where I can escape the madness of Willoughby!" he often said.

He used it to practice his violin, compose new pieces of music, and avoid all the wearisome characters he knew around town.

Despite the fact that he went to his cottage to hide out, however, Uncle Maynard did also have several friends on or near the lake. So he was very familiar with the terrain, and there might also be someone there who could help them. Still, as Uncle Maynard drove the two young people home after their visit to City Hall, the matter at hand was taking his medicine and resting for a while.

"I'm sorry to say that I'm going to be quite a drag on our plans," he said. "If only I were young again."

William smiled, but the fact was that he was a bit worried. He had seen his uncle in various states of ill health for as long as he had known him. But this time things did seem a bit more serious. William had never quite seen his uncle's skin turn this shade of white before. It looked like the glistening edge of a porcelain sink rather than human flesh. Of course, few things upset Uncle Maynard more than foolish people with lots of power, so perhaps his physical state was little more than the result of their run-in with the mayor. It was difficult to say.

At any rate, following fifteen minutes of Uncle Maynard's terrifying driving (during which Sophie complained exactly twelve times), they finally made it home. And after they managed to work their way through the mansion's various security systems, Uncle Maynard quickly went upstairs to take his medication. This took about ten minutes. And soon, he arrived back in the kitchen looking a little better.

"I think I'll be all right now," he said to William and Sophie as he opened up the refrigerator. "Now, let's have something to eat while we talk about Starling Lake."

Lunch was leftovers from the previous night's lasagna, and after they commenced eating, they began to discuss their next steps, although their plan was fairly firm. They'd go to Starling Lake, try to sneak into the mayor's mansion, and, if all went well, find a way to set Sophie's parents free.

Uncle Maynard did suggest one more time that he might still be able to reason with the mayor. "I just can't accept that Preston would treat me like this," he said, shaking his head and putting a forkful of lasagna in his mouth. Still, they all decided that at this point, they couldn't trust Uncle Maynard's powers of persuasion over the mayor again.

"If we get caught, you should try talking to him again," Sophie said. "But I think we just need to sneak in, get my parents, and sneak out without anyone finding out."

"I hope it will be that easy," William added as he bit into a large, flopping noodle.

"Well no one will be expecting us," Uncle Maynard said. "I can't imagine they think anyone's going to raid the mayor's mansion. That's the good thing about hanging around with aliens. You can count on people staying away from you." Here, Uncle Maynard sighed. "I just think it would be better if at least one of us had some experience with this kind of thing. A sick old man and two young people hardly seems like the best team for this."

"We can manage," William responded, thinking that his confident attitude might somehow impress Sophie and his uncle. They seemed, however, mostly unimpressed. William looked at his uncle, who now looked slightly puzzled. And Sophie too seemed lost in thought, and, in fact, looked somewhat depressed as far as William could tell.

"I'm sure they're all right," William finally said to Sophie. "Your parents. I'm sure they're all right. And I'm sure we'll be able to find them and get them out of whatever trouble they're in."

Sophie looked at William and forced a smile. She

had a forkful of lasagna suspended in front of her. "I just want to get them out and head north to the Northern Empire," she said. "We can't come back here. They'll only be caught again."

William paused for a moment, and for the first time he wondered if he and his uncle ought to think about making the journey north as well.

Uncle Maynard read William's mind.

"We're coming back here," he said. "Preston Walters isn't going to give us any trouble. He might be a bit angry if he finds out that we helped set the doctors free. But he'll get over it. This is home, William. And I'm too old to leave. Perhaps you can go, if that's what you want. But I think we'll be just fine back here."

The thought of being separated from Uncle Maynard now was unthinkable to William. "No, I want to stay with you," he said firmly, although it did occur to him that life might not actually be so easy for them back in Willoughby if they succeeded with their rescue attempt.

Lunch was soon finished, and as Uncle Maynard and Sophie started on the dishes, William began playing the violin (with occasional corrections from Uncle Maynard). They'd leave later that afternoon. Starling Lake was two hours away. They decided they wanted to arrive just as night was falling. They'd regroup at Uncle Maynard's cottage, and then head to the mayor's mansion by boat late at night.

"I know any number of people who will lend us a boat," Uncle Maynard said after drying a large plate. "I think, however, that the one we should use is one we'll have to steal. But it will be easy enough. And it won't really be stealing. It will be more like borrowing."

This seemed reasonable to William, who had decided in the previous moment that the entire idea of trying to sneak past the mayor and a bunch of aliens was already a crazy plan. How could stealing a boat make it any worse?

"Now, I think I need a short nap," Uncle Maynard said, putting down his dish towel and stretching. "I'm useless without an afternoon nap."

William well knew that this was true. "While you're lying down, we'll pack up enough food for a couple of days," he said. "Who knows how long we'll be up there?"

"And let's bring some frozen lasagnas!" Uncle Maynard called behind him as he headed toward the back hall. "I'll be back in about an hour to see how you're coming along."

And with that, he disappeared up the stairs.

William looked over at Sophie to see if she seemed any less depressed. But he wasn't exactly sure how she felt because she just looked at him like she often looked at him in school–in that somewhat amused and baffled way, like he was very, very strange. And William looked back at her like he normally did–like this was the most appealing young woman he had ever seen and he was terrified that she was about to make fun of him.

But then something odd happened.

Sophie flashed him a very warm smile and said, "You know, I really appreciate all this, William. You're a very odd person. And your uncle is the very strangest man I've ever met. But I really appreciate all this. I feel like you're doing so much for me–things that you don't have to do at all."

William looked back at Sophie, now slightly confused about how he ought to behave. He felt, in fact, that he ought to say something heroic and extremely manly. But such things never came easily for William, and instead he just quietly said, "You're welcome." And in the next instant, he was trying to distract himself with the frozen lasagnas, planning out the best way to pack them.

15

The rules of the peace were clear. They applied only to the city of Willoughby. And as William, Sophie, and Uncle Maynard drove past the city limits and into the depths of Blackthorne Forest (the enormous forest that surrounded Willoughby), they all understood that the so-called peace no longer applied and that they were now in more dangerous territory.

"Of course, this peace is nonsense," Uncle Maynard said. "But it might at least have prevented aliens from devouring us in broad daylight. Now we don't even have that protection."

"Thanks for pointing that out," Sophie said, looking nervously out her window.

"Well, it's always best to be brutally honest at a time like this," Uncle Maynard replied. "No point in sugarcoating anything. That's the surest way to run into trouble."

William thought about this as they wound their way through the shadowy, snaking road deep in the forest bed and concluded that he much preferred sugarcoating the truth to facing it head-on. As he looked up at the tree canopy and glimpsed small bursts of light piercing the leaf cover, he decided that he'd actually really prefer to be in his attic at that moment, puzzling over some kind of complicated sheet music. "I think we're safer here than in most places, though," he finally said, still looking up at the trees. "I'll bet it would be hard for the aliens to get their aircraft in here–beneath all these trees."

"You're probably right about that, William," Uncle Maynard replied, looking into his rearview mirror. (William was in the backseat.) "Good point."

And it was a good point. Driving along a winding road at the bottom of a forest would probably be a good thing to do if alien aircraft were threatening you. The problem was that although this was clear-headed reasoning on William's part, it turned out not actually to be true. About an hour into their journey, they suddenly heard the strange whistling and thumping noise of one of the alien aircraft, and after a few seconds, the lone aircraft came buzzing from behind them and passed right over their heads.

It was going very quickly, and just kept on going after it passed. A relief for everyone. But about one hundred yards ahead of them, it suddenly slowed and came to a halt, hovering in midair.

"OK, what's going on here?" Uncle Maynard said, stopping the car.

The aircraft spun around and faced them directly, its strange metal outcroppings branching in all directions.

Sophie, William, and Uncle Maynard had not labored too long with packing that afternoon, but they had remembered the essentials–flashlights, violins, lasagnas, etc. At the top of their list, though, were three of the alien guns that Uncle Maynard had on hand, and at this point they were all relieved to have them in the car.

"Move slowly," Uncle Maynard said, "but I think we should each grab hold of a gun right now." He reached behind him to the seat next to William, where the guns were. "But no one panic. Let's wait for a moment, until we figure out what they want."

"I think they want to eat us," William said as he lifted his gun onto his lap.

The guns were large but not very heavy, being made from some kind of alien material that weighed next to nothing. Because they were large, however, they were slightly difficult to aim and shoot. But they were effective, and they had a dial that adjusted the charge–from light stun to violent death beam. William decided that violent death beam was probably the best setting for this occasion.

"What are they doing?" Sophie said.

The aircraft was still not moving. It simply hovered in the air. All of a sudden, though, the aircraft dropped until it was ten feet off the ground, then sped forward, making a terrifying rattle.

Uncle Maynard opened his door slightly. Sophie and William did the same.

The aircraft came to another abrupt halt. It was now only forty feet away.

Our three friends slowly slid out of the car and crouched behind the two open front doors.

"No sudden moves," Uncle Maynard whispered, his voice sounding very serious. "But I don't think we should try to negotiate. If they get out, open fire. But wait till they all get out. No firing till we see them all. They're not going to blow us up yet. It wouldn't help them any to blow us up."

And this was, in fact, true. One of the advantages of being food was that the aliens weren't likely to blow you up. That is, if they blew you to bits, they couldn't really eat you. Still, the aircraft continued to hover in place.

"I want to know what they're doing," Sophie said.

"It's very difficult to know," Uncle Maynard replied.

Suddenly the aircraft dropped to the ground. It hissed as the engine slowed to a halt. Then a large black door abruptly opened. An instant passed. Then another instant. And then an alien stepped out. Its drooling mouth snarled at the three humans. Its tentacles waved wildly above it. And its robotic leggings hissed slightly as they slowly stepped forward.

"Wait for his friends to leave the ship before we start shooting," Uncle Maynard whispered. "We want to get them all."

As he said this, two more aliens began to get out.

But as this happened, a new strange whistling sounded from behind them. When they turned to see what it was, another alien aircraft appeared in the distance, and it was flying straight toward them.

"OK," Uncle Maynard said. "No time to wait now. Fire!"

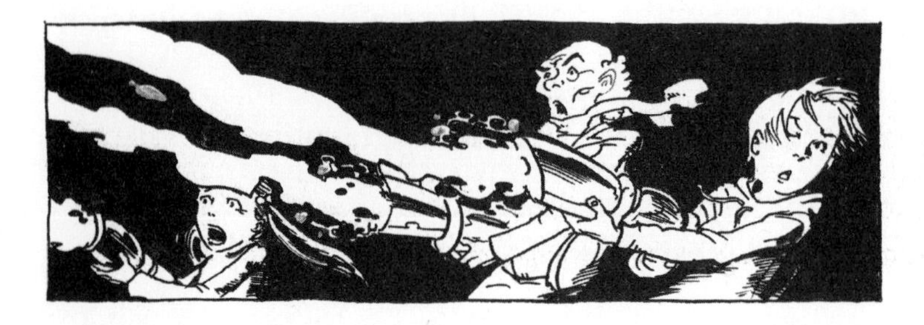

Suddenly, bursts of electricity shot from our three heroes' guns. Two of the aliens quickly fell to the ground in twitching masses of green flesh. The other was only slightly wounded. It started getting back inside the aircraft. William took careful aim. In the next instant he shot it right in the back. It lurched forward, still trying to get inside. But Uncle Maynard and Sophie both got off shots. The alien suddenly fell back in a flash of electricity, smoldering and motionless, its robotic leggings twisting and kicking, almost as if they were still trying to escape.

It was a striking moment. And the truth was that it was a thing that William would remember for the rest of his life–killing another living being, albeit an evil and threatening one. Frankly, he felt wretched. But sorting out his feelings about the nature of life and death would have to wait. The other alien aircraft was bearing down on them.

"Turn around!" Uncle Maynard yelled.

The three quickly turned and stared at the other aircraft.

"We'll be in range in two seconds," Uncle Maynard said.

"One, two . . . *now!*"

Suddenly another volley of electric flashes burst through the air, catching the aircraft's shining black underbelly. The aircraft swerved slightly, then steadied itself. Uncle Maynard quickly pulled his gun back and shot at the left wing. The beam hit a long metal fin. They heard a loud snap. All at once, the aircraft lurched into a violent spin. It spun for a brief instant at an enormous speed, firing several large electric bombs into the treetops of Blackthorne Forest. Then it pitched forward again, right toward the car.

"Move!" Uncle Maynard yelled. The three of them dove to the sides of the road.

The aircraft continued forward, right at the car. But at the last minute, it pulled up. It rose slightly and missed the car by just a few inches. It continued forward, right toward the other aircraft. It was still out of control, but it tried to pull up farther. This time, however, it didn't make it. It went crashing into the other aircraft forty feet away, exploding on impact into a gigantic ball of fire.

William, Sophie, and Uncle Maynard were now all lying with their heads down. William stared at the ground for a moment, and then finally looked up to see a mass of flames. As the fire burst upward and the explosion seemed to grow, William felt enveloped by an astonishing kind of numbness–or a kind of motionlessness–lit by orange flames that now cast their terrifying light across the faces of Sophie and

Uncle Maynard. They were just beyond the danger. It was only light from the flames. But for a moment, William felt as though he were being swallowed by a noiseless fire. He couldn't hear a thing. He seemed to be surrounded by silence. Everything was in silent slow motion–slow motion lit by this strange orange flame.

It seemed they were safe though. William continued to try to get his bearings. He was trying to grasp what had just happened. The sense of relief was like a strange kind of sleep, keeping his mind far away from the danger.

But then, just as suddenly, there was a burst from an alien gun about twenty feet away.

William looked slightly to his left. One of the aliens–half-burned–was staggering forward, shooting wildly at them.

They all reached down for their guns. William got to his first. He brought the gun forward, took aim, and launched a beam of electricity right into the chest of the alien. The damage was swift. The alien fell instantly. This time, it would not be getting back up.

William looked back and forth at Sophie and his uncle, trying to comprehend what had just happened. And then, all at once, the spell of silence broke, and a rush of noise enveloped William with a deafening roar. William could hear nothing but the roar of the fire. It seemed to last forever. His uncle grabbed his shoulder and yelled something. But William couldn't hear what he was saying. Nothing. All he could make out was the roar and the light. Finally, though, with his uncle's mouth next to his ear, William heard, "We've got to go!"

William looked at him. He was still painted with the same bright light from the flames. It was all so confusing. But William understood.

"Okay," William said at last. He pushed his gun forward and crouched. Then he stood up and slowly began walking forward. Sophie followed. And Uncle

Maynard came close behind. In the next moment, they were all back inside the car.

They sat for just a second, each looking back and forth at one another.

But they had to keep moving.

"We have to go," Uncle Maynard said finally. "These aliens may have friends nearby." Uncle Maynard took a deep breath and turned on the car. The two alien aircraft were still burning. But Uncle Maynard was able to drive by them on a patch of dirt to the right of the road. Before long, William, Sophie, and Uncle Maynard resumed their journey down the dark road, deep below the canopy of Blackthorne Forest.

16

It took another hour to make it to Uncle Maynard's cottage, and the trip passed anxiously. They were all relieved to have escaped from the aliens. But at every turn they wondered if there would be more waiting for them. It was surprising that they had survived at all. They knew that they had been very lucky. It was rare for humans to have alien guns. No doubt the aliens were shocked when our three heroes started firing at them. Still, things could easily have gone the other way.

There was also the question of alien friends. Maybe more aliens were on their way to punish the three for what they had done. But as Uncle Maynard and William and Sophie finally began the drive down the narrow and grass-covered road that led to the cottage, they decided that they were probably safe.

"I think we'll be all right now," Uncle Maynard

said. "I think that no aliens will be coming after us at this point." Still as William, Sophie, and Uncle Maynard came to a halt before Uncle Maynard's stone cottage, they all agreed that they had to be very careful from now on. "After all, the most difficult things are yet to come," Uncle Maynard said. "But I think we should be pretty pleased with ourselves. I feel like we passed some kind of test."

"Yeah. I think we did pretty well," Sophie agreed. And then she looked over toward William and smiled.

It occurred to William again that it was very strange to have Sophie look upon him as anything more than a ridiculous and incompetent boy. It was quite astonishing, in fact, this new way she had of smiling at him, and after a moment of confusion, he started to blush. But the blush was only for an instant. He still couldn't get over the idea that he had really killed another living being, although he did manage to push this fact far back into the more murky recesses of his mind.

At any rate, as far as secluded country homes went, Uncle Maynard's was something close to perfect. It was made from large oak beams and smooth stones that had been found in Blackthorne Forest and along the Blackthorne River. William had been there many times, especially when he was younger and his parents were still alive. There was a large apple orchard behind the cottage, where Uncle Maynard had first taught him to play the violin. It was here that Uncle Maynard had himself learned to play the violin when he was a boy, and the land and the cottage belonged to his own father. It was a wonderful place, and visiting it always meant a great deal to William, as it did to Uncle Maynard. In fact, as William stopped unpacking for a moment and looked into the apple trees (now set against a darkening sky), Uncle Maynard came up behind him, put his hand on William's shoulder, and said, "It will be nice to come back here again after this is all over. It's normally such a happy place."

It was a happy place, and it hurt William to think about how distant that world seemed to him now. He looked at the orchard, and at the cottage, and at the old blue truck that Uncle Maynard kept there for various bits of work he did on his land. It was all so strange. Even though he was standing right there, the whole scene still seemed to be very, very far away.

"You and your parents can take this truck when you head north," Uncle Maynard suddenly called out to Sophie. "Or we can steal you something. But this is a good truck. And I've got some canisters of gasoline in the back. So it should take you pretty far."

Sophie walked up behind them. "Thanks," she said. "I don't know what to say."

"Well, you're welcome to it. I'm glad it will be useful."

Sophie started to thank Uncle Maynard again, but he quickly interrupted. "Okay," he said, "let's finish unloading."

The interior of Uncle Maynard's cottage was much like the exterior. It was lined with stones and wooden beams and had a gigantic main room that served as a living room, dining room, and kitchen. It had a high, vaulted ceiling, and its thick wooden rafters stretched gracefully between the opposite angled planes of the roof. The kitchen area consisted of a large stove, various appliances, and an enormous stone counter.

It looked like a cottage and felt like a cottage, but,

frankly, it was too big and too well made to be quite the real thing. Instead, it was obviously the country home of a man who was from the city and wealthy enough to build whatever pleased him. And it was definitely the home of a man who enjoyed solitude. The cottage had been built all by itself on the edge of the apple orchard, rather than on Starling Lake, where motorboats and water-skiers were always zooming by. It was quite clear that no one ever made it to this part of the area.

"I bet you never see anyone out here," Sophie said as she stepped through the doorway.

"Not unless I want to," Uncle Maynard replied.

After unpacking, and lighting a large fire in the fireplace, Uncle Maynard suggested that they have dinner.

He walked to the kitchen counter and stated with great conviction and resolution that his very favorite food was lasagna. "My very favorite food is lasagna!" he said. He then unpacked a frozen lasagna from the cooler and popped it into the oven.

"Lasagna!" he said again. "I can't wait."

Sophie looked at William and smiled. Again, it was

a kind of smile that William was hardly used to–from her, at any rate. He again tried not to blush. And he succeeded to a certain extent. He just turned a light shade of red, smiled back, and then walked over to the fire. The cottage was cold, and he needed to warm himself up.

17

Uncle Maynard had a friend who had a large house on the lake. "A good friend," he said, "who has unfortunately been eaten."

This good friend had a family, though, who did not much care for Uncle Maynard, and he concluded that they ought not to interact with them at all. "We do need to use their boat, though," Uncle Maynard said.

(They were now at the kitchen table, finishing their lasagna.)

"Or, we need to steal it, that is," Uncle Maynard continued. "But it might not be such a problem. Who knows where the family is? They might still be in Willoughby. Or they also might have been dinner for some horde of aliens. It's impossible to say. But we do need their boat."

The advantage of this boat, Uncle Maynard

explained, was that it was electric. That meant that they didn't have to deal with any noisy gasoline engines that might wake up security guards. And the electric motor also meant they wouldn't have to do any rowing.

"Given my poor health," Uncle Maynard said, happily scooping lasagna into his mouth, "that's entirely out of the question."

The house of the now-eaten friend (who happened to be named Carlyle Finneman) was on the opposite side of the lake from the mayor's. It was about a twenty-minute boat ride from end to end in the electric boat, which, like all boats with electric motors, did not go very fast.

"Of course, we could try to sneak in on foot," Uncle Maynard added. "But there's only one road into the mayor's place. And if we took a back route, it would be about a three-mile hike through dense forest. We'd definitely get lost. And that would be if we were lucky. If we were unlucky, a couple of the mayor's henchmen would find us and shoot us on the spot. They might even torture us first. Or turn us into a kind of snack for creatures from outer space."

Sophie jerked back slightly as Uncle Maynard said this, and looked like she was about to say something, when William jumped in. "Okay. The boat sounds best," he agreed, stabbing a large noodle with his fork. "And we all think that we should go tonight? Get started right away?"

"Well, I'm usually in favor of taking lots of time to plan things out," Uncle Maynard replied. "But I think so. I think we should go tonight. There's no reason not to. There's nothing really preventing us from getting started. All we need to do is sneak into the Finneman house and steal the boat keys. I know where they are, so it shouldn't be too hard, and I know where he keeps the key to the back door. In fact, I know everything about the place, given all the times I've hung around with Carlyle Finneman. Carlyle and I got along very well, despite how everyone else in his family felt about me."

Uncle Maynard paused, and then laughed. "Of course, maybe none of this matters too much anyway," he said. "This time tomorrow, we might be flowing through the digestive systems of aliens!"

Uncle Maynard laughed even harder as he said

this, but the two young people didn't find this idea very funny. William looked sideways at a now slightly angry Sophie. Uncle Maynard caught his glance.

"I suppose I shouldn't make that kind of joke. I keep forgetting that you're much younger than I am. I suppose if you always feel like you're on the edge of death, alien digestive juices don't scare you as much. But, of course, such a thing isn't a bit funny. Especially for young people. Now, I'm exhausted! Let's take a short nap and then get ready to go. We should leave here about two a.m. and try to make it to the mayor's around four. Everyone should be asleep then. Sound good?"

William nodded, and said, "Okay."

Sophie did the same.

18

So, it was an evening of restless napping, but before long our heroes were finally ready to head to the mayor's. They prepared somewhat, but there really was not too much to do, and soon William, Sophie, and Uncle Maynard were in the car and pulling away from Uncle Maynard's cottage.

It should be noted once again that the mayor's mansion on Starling Lake was more than just a house. It was really more of a compound. That is, it consisted of several buildings built on a big piece of land on the lake's shore. It even had a name–it was called Blackthorne Lodge.

Among the buildings at Blackthorne Lodge was a stable (for the mayor's expensive horses); an indoor swimming pool and gymnasium (where the mayor performed his daily exercises); a guest cottage (for mothers-in-law, loud children, and other distracting guests); the mansion (something close to a modern-day castle); and (as previously mentioned) a large laboratory in the renovated barn, where, years earlier, the mayor's father developed new uses for the extra-strong, lightweight plastic bags that first made him his fortune.

As Uncle Maynard carefully drove through the quiet road between his cottage and the Finneman home, he tried to detail these various buildings as best as he could.

"There's also a boathouse," he said. "It's very large, holds four boats, and it has an extremely pleasant upstairs game room. As I remember, security guards like to hang around there, and I can't imagine it will be any different tonight."

"How many times have you been there?" Sophie asked.

"In recent years, only twice," he replied. "But when Preston's father was alive, I was a regular guest. Of course, in those days it was a bit more modest. I mean, it was still something of a palace. But a more modest palace. The racehorses, the indoor swimming facilities, and so on, are all new. And there were no security guards running around back then either."

"Did you like his father?" William asked.

"Indeed I did. He was an extremely strange individual. But he was smart as a whip, and a very decent human being. He only ever liked to do two things: experiment in his lab and sit by the lake with friends. You can't help but respect a man with such straightforward interests."

"How did the mayor turn out like he did?"

"Well, that's a little more difficult to say. I got to know him when I tried teaching him to play the violin, but I didn't get to know him as well as you might think. He was extremely lazy, and he always wanted something for nothing. For instance, he wanted to be a good violin player, but he could never accept how much work it took to become one. I will say this, however: he loved his father just about more than any boy I've ever seen. He was absolutely devastated when he died. Preston was a grown man, but it was a terrible thing to watch him face that loss. That says something about his character, although I'm not sure what. On balance, I'd say we shouldn't trust him one bit. But he did love his father. I can say that."

Uncle Maynard sighed as he came to the end of

this little discussion, and then made a sharp left turn down a road that was even more narrow than the last. Before leaving that night, he and William had put black tape across the brake lights, and part of each headlight, to hide their presence as much as possible. Some light escaped. It was pitch-black out, and without it, they never would have been able to follow the road. But now that they were driving through a maze of bushes, they could hardly see two feet ahead of them. Finally, Uncle Maynard veered right slightly, pulled alongside an enormous juniper bush, and turned off the engine.

"We're about a quarter mile from the Finneman house now," he said. "We should walk from here. We don't want them to spot us, if there's anyone home."

This seemed like a good plan to William and Sophie, and they were soon walking through the woods, barely able to see anything. Fortunately, the forest thinned as they approached the lake, and a half moon was just rising–enough to see by, but not really enough for them to get spotted. They'd brought flashlights, too, just in case. But they were only for emergencies. Flashlights would be a pretty quick signal of their whereabouts to anyone who might be after them.

Eventually, they began to make out the dark rim of a large house. It had a broad, swooping roof, which seemed to drift gently into the surrounding trees. It was hard to make out too much detail, though, because it was dark and there were no lights on inside, which was, in fact, good news.

"No lights!" Uncle Maynard said, stopping for a moment. "I don't think anyone is there. This is good luck."

Uncle Maynard had just begun to walk again, when suddenly (and somewhat ironically) a light came on in the kitchen.

"Hang on!" Uncle Maynard said in a whisper.

They stopped and crouched down, staring at the lit window.

There was nothing to see at first, but before long, they saw a short man in a bathrobe stumble toward the refrigerator. He opened it, looked up and down for a moment, took out what looked like a large, cold turkey, and closed the door again.

"Midnight snack!" Uncle Maynard whispered. "No problem. We'll wait him out."

"At least we know that someone's home," Sophie said.

"Yes. But that's Carlyle's son-in-law. I can't say he likes me very much. He's the new owner, I suppose, now that Carlyle has been eaten."

William wanted to ask what, exactly, this son-in-law disliked about Uncle Maynard, but it seemed that at this particular moment, the matter was best left alone.

It took about ten minutes for the man to finish his snack (which eventually included cheese, orange juice, olives, a large yellow Popsicle, and an entire turkey leg). Finally, after inspecting the refrigerator one last time, he shut the door, turned off the light, and disappeared.

"The boat keys are kept in the kitchen," Uncle Maynard whispered, "on a little rack not far from the back door. They won't be hard to get. Let's give it another five minutes. Then we'll go in. He should be back asleep by then, given how much he's eaten. But even if he's not asleep, he won't hear us if we're careful."

Five minutes passed. Following the wait, they started toward the house again. William put his alien gun over his shoulder, using a strap that attached from the stock to the barrel. He was happy it was so light, although it was still quite large.

When they arrived at the edge of the driveway, Uncle Maynard began whispering again. "I think, actually, you two should just wait here," he said. "Let me go in alone and grab the boat keys. Keep things simple. I'll meet you back here in two minutes. Don't move."

Uncle Maynard quietly walked down the driveway. There were several steps leading to the door. He walked up them silently. Then he took hold of the door knob and slowly turned it. He pushed gently on the door, careful not to make any noise.

But the pushing didn't do any good.

The door wouldn't move.

It was locked.

Uncle Maynard paused for a second. Then he quickly put his hand above the door. He felt around on a small ledge, just above the doorway. But he found nothing. He paused again, and then began to move his hand once more. He felt above the ledge, and then slid a broken shingle to one side. His hand moved slightly. Then it dropped back down. He turned back to the two young people and held up a key in the moonlight. In the next instant, he unlocked the back door and stepped into the kitchen.

All seemed to be going well. But after a few minutes, Uncle Maynard failed to reappear. He was inside the darkened downstairs for about five minutes before William began to feel worried.

"He said the keys would be easy to find," he said to Sophie.

"I'm sure he knows where they are," she replied. "He knew where the house key was."

Still, it was troubling.

Suddenly, a small light came on. It surprised William at first, but then he realized it was Uncle Maynard's flashlight. It was risky. But clearly Uncle Maynard couldn't find the keys without it. After a few more minutes, the flashlight shut off, and Uncle Maynard reappeared at the back door. He paused, then quickly darted across the driveway.

"They're not there!" he whispered as he arrived next to the young people. "I have to check a few more places. Wait here." Then Uncle Maynard turned,

strode across the driveway again, and disappeared back inside.

William looked at Sophie, barely making her out in the dim moonlight. She looked back at him and said, "I really hope he finds them."

The next several minutes passed silently. Each moment William hoped that Uncle Maynard would appear at the door. But there was only darkness and silence, strange insects fluttering by in the darkness, and the strong smell of pine from the trees above. The waiting was agonizing, and somehow William's surroundings grew more and more frightening. Not finding the boat keys would put a swift end to their plan. William, in fact, began to try to think up alternate strategies. Maybe they would have to steal someone else's boat. Or maybe they could start the boat without the keys, although he didn't exactly know how they'd manage that. William was at a loss. He just kept staring hopefully at the door, thinking his uncle would arrive any minute.

And then, suddenly, a very unexpected thing happened. An extremely loud crashing noise came from inside. William thought it sounded like an entire chest of drawers had tipped over. And it sounded like its top had been covered with brass trinkets and china figurines. And maybe two or three very large lamps.

"I don't think this is going very well," William said to Sophie, now catching his breath. In the next instant, the lights came on.

"This way," William said, grabbing Sophie's hand and pulling her back to the bushes. Suddenly they heard a man's voice scream, "Who's there? I've got a shotgun! Who's there? You'd better leave now because I've got a gun, and I'll shoot you dead!"

"I don't think I can take this," Sophie said, stepping very close to William.

"Me neither," William replied.

The man's screaming continued. He was mostly yelling various sorts of threats. "You filthy animals," he kept saying. "Come into my home and I'll kill you. I'll kill you all, you filthy aliens." This continued for some time. He kept repeating the same things, obsessed with insulting the aliens' poor sense of hygiene and lack of common decency. And then, just as quickly, there was silence. Total silence.

The silence lasted for what seemed like hours.

And then there was some scratching.

And then a large thump.

And then, suddenly, in the next instant, the gun went off. "BANG!"

And then it went off again. "BANG!"

Sophie grabbed hold of William's arm, but she didn't say a word.

William wanted to say something that might restore some kind of calm, but the fact of the matter was that he was panicking. He simply grabbed hold of Sophie's other arm and began squeezing it, too.

"We have to go in there," Sophie said at last. "We have to help him."

"Okay. Okay," William replied. "Let's think for just a minute. We can't lose our heads. We have to have a plan."

But William couldn't come up with a reasonable

course of action. Should they challenge the anxious Finneman son-in-law and try to overpower him? They had their own guns–alien guns that would probably scare the poor man out of his mind. But did they really want a shoot-out? William didn't think he could shoot a person. It wasn't like shooting at an alien, and that, he now knew, was extremely difficult, despite the fact that aliens made a point of eating everyone in sight. But they had to do something. They had to save his uncle.

"Grab your gun and let's go," William finally said. "We've got to go in."

"All right," Sophie said.

William was terrified. And he could sense that Sophie was too. She was breathing very rapidly and kept muttering, "Okay, okay, we'll be okay" under her breath.

Slowly, they crept along the driveway to the back door. As they approached the edge of the house, the man reappeared, now standing in the kitchen window once more, with his profile to William and Sophie. He looked terrified, and he had the shotgun to his shoulder. He wasn't looking outside. But they had to be careful. They couldn't let him see them.

But it was a puzzle. What was next?

The man wasn't screaming anymore. He was stone silent. But he was scared stiff and looked very confused. William and Sophie were side by side, staring into the window and creeping slowly toward the door.

Suddenly, a hand clamped down on William's shoulder. He turned quickly, gasping and ready to fire. But there, in the dim moonlight, he saw his uncle.

"I've got them!" Uncle Maynard quickly said.

"What happened?" Sophie snapped, also quite surprised.

"Shhhh!" Uncle Maynard said.

William looked back at the window, but the man hadn't heard her. He was still looking around, panicked, waving his shotgun up and down. Then he started yelling again. "I'm ready for you!" he screamed. "No one's eating me. I'll tell you that right now, you horrible beasts."

"I came out the other door," Uncle Maynard whispered. "But let's go back here." He darted back across the driveway and into another patch of small trees, farther away from the house. William and Sophie followed.

"Let's just stay here for a bit," Uncle Maynard said, crouching behind a large bush. "Let him calm down. He'll lock himself in his room in a few minutes. He'll hide there. He's a very nervous man. Very jumpy! Not a reasonable man at all. We can go in a few minutes, after things have settled."

They waited for five minutes. Finally, the man disappeared from the kitchen window. A moment passed, and then a light came on in a small room on the top floor.

"He's going to hide in the attic," Uncle Maynard said. "The poor man. He probably thought he was safe up here at the lake." Uncle Maynard chuckled a little, then stepped away from the bush to get a better look into the kitchen window.

"He's gone," he said. "I'm sure that's him in the attic. He won't be down soon, what with all these man-eating aliens running about. Let's go!"

Uncle Maynard turned and headed down toward the boathouse. William and Sophie followed.

19

Starling Lake was about twenty-five square miles, which is actually not that big when it comes to lakes–only about four miles across one way and eight the other, with lots of outcroppings and craggy shores. Still, as William looked across the dark body of water, their destination seemed very far away.

They paused a moment to take it all in, and then Uncle Maynard pointed to a spot just below the moon. "That's about where the mayor's mansion is," he said, his long arm lit by the moonlight. There were a few dim lights shining from that direction. "I

assume most of the people there are asleep," he continued. "But someone will be up. You can count on that. The one thing we have going for us is that they probably won't be expecting midnight interlopers. Who in their right mind would sneak into a camp filled with thugs and aliens? Anyone with any sense is back in Willoughby, cowering in their bedrooms. We must be crazy!"

Uncle Maynard laughed a little, told the young people to follow him, and then led the way into the boathouse and onto the electric boat.

As far as William could tell, the electric boat was not difficult to drive. It was just like any other boat, except that it had a nearly silent electric motor powering the propeller. After unplugging it, Uncle Maynard started it up and backed it out of its slip with ease. It was slow. But, again, it was quiet, which was most important.

"This is just the way to tool around the lake at cocktail hour," Uncle Maynard said. He reached up and tapped the large wooden frame that arched across the boat and over the passengers' heads. The frame was open–you could see the sky–but there was a canvas top in the back that could be pulled over the frame in case of rain.

"Maybe one day when all this madness passes, we can meet up here and really enjoy ourselves," Uncle Maynard continued.

"If that day ever comes, I don't know what I'll do," Sophie said. "I'm just hoping there's a little hut for us in the Northern Empire."

"I'm sure they have lake houses up there," Uncle Maynard said. "They can't have torn them all down just because a few aliens showed up."

"I just want to go home and practice my violin," William said.

"I think this can only help you, William," Uncle Maynard replied, the moon catching his face as he looked toward the shore. "It's no good for an artist to be locked up in an attic. An artist has to go on adventures. And you can hardly beat this one. You fought aliens today, after all."

William considered this, and said, "I can't believe that was just this afternoon. It seems like years ago."

"It does indeed," Uncle Maynard said.

William thought for a moment about what would

be next for him, and he slowly began to feel very sad that Sophie might be heading north. The water slapped against the boat and made a gentle, rhythmic sound, causing William to feel just a bit contemplative. He was sitting next to Sophie, and being near her gave him a strange kind of comfort–not the sort of thing he was used to with her. He had so few real friends, it seemed to him, and now the person he most wanted to be close to was leaving.

As he looked over at Sophie, he thought about trying to talk his uncle into going north as well. After tonight, they might have no choice. But he had a hard time imagining his uncle agreeing to starting a new life in the Northern Empire. He'd probably want to fight it out at his house in Willoughby rather than be chased away by aliens or the mayor. And then, William thought about his brother, and what things must be like for him in Great Harbor. William considered his own circumstances, and his now-eaten stepparents, and thought that he would definitely try again to contact his brother once they were back in Willoughby, if indeed they ever got back there. Perhaps they had rigged up some sort of new phone system at the so-called Temporary Emergency Center that he could use, or even a temporary mail system that some intrepid postal carrier had tried to start. One way or another, though, William had to figure out a way to find out if he was all right.

William, Sophie, and Uncle Maynard continued traveling in silence for about another ten minutes. William was deep in thought. The water kept its perfect and regular rhythm, slapping against the boat. The electric motor also made just a little noise. Not anything close to a roar. Just a very quiet, pleasant hum.

Finally, Uncle Maynard broke the silence. "We're about halfway there," he said. "From here on out, only whispering. Sound carries very well on water. We don't want to let anyone know we're here."

"Okay," Sophie replied. William said the same.

They traveled along the shore to make navigation easier, but it also happened to be the shorter route because of the way the lake was shaped. And it seemed good to stay along the tree-lined shore, because it was harder to be spotted, although they were pretty sure that no one was watching.

As they finally got closer to the mayor's compound, several lights were burning at various places on the property. William began to wonder where they would land, when suddenly the boat veered left.

Uncle Maynard whispered, "I think we should come ashore right about there–out at that end of the property–before we get too close. There probably won't be anyone poking around out there."

They were now able to see the compound much more clearly. The moonlight glistened off the rooftops and the leafy autumn trees swayed in the wind. The barn that had been converted into the laboratory sat far at the other end of the property, and they could tell that there were several lights on inside.

As for security guards wandering the grounds, they hadn't spotted any yet. And it was pretty certain no one could see them. Anyway, it wasn't like anyone was looking for them. Their arrival was probably the very last thing on the mind of the mayor and anyone else at the compound.

"This really is quite crazy of us," Uncle Maynard whispered. They were pulling closer to the shore.

"It's too late now," William replied in a hushed voice.

Slowly they came closer to land. They were still

some distance from the buildings. Finally, they approached a large, uprooted tree that jutted into the water. Uncle Maynard brought the boat alongside the tree and guided it to a small, sandy beach that was about twenty feet wide.

"Make as little noise as possible when you get out," Uncle Maynard said at a volume so low that William and Sophie could barely hear him. The bottom of the boat began to scrape gently against the sandy lake bed.

"Here we are," Uncle Maynard said. "I'll tie it to the tree trunk. Remember your guns."

William and Sophie carefully stepped out of the boat and onto the sandy shore. Uncle Maynard finished tying off the boat, and then he followed, slinging his gun over his shoulder.

20

The path leading up to the lodge lay beneath large, drooping oak trees, and on either side of the path there were unpruned bushes hanging onto the ground. The bushes were thick. And there was a breeze rustling through them. So it was good cover–it would be very hard to see or hear Uncle Maynard and the two young people as they stalked toward the compound.

The first of the buildings at Blackthorne, the guest cottage, was about five hundred feet away, so they were still some distance from any activity.

"But we have to be as quiet as possible," Uncle Maynard whispered. "I'm sure there are guards on patrol."

"Okay," William and Sophie said quietly.

Uncle Maynard then ducked his head and led the way, carefully stepping along the bushes that grew on either side of the narrow path.

They made it up the pathway without any problems and were soon about fifty feet from the guest cottage–a large, white, two-story house in which a family of eight would be very comfortable. There was a single light inside, although they couldn't see anything through the window yet. There was another bright light shining off the roof, pointed onto the ground below. It meant that they couldn't cut in front of the building–they would have to go around back.

"Good enough," Uncle Maynard whispered. "Best to stay close to the trees anyway." The cottage sat in what they could now see was a huge mowed lawn that connected all of the buildings. At the edge of the lawn, around the perimeter of the compound, there were large patches of woods. If they stayed behind the buildings, they could easily sneak along these wooded patches that surrounded the compound. In fact, the woods were dark enough, and the compound appeared to be so deserted, that it didn't seem like it would be any problem at all. It actually occurred to William that they might be back to the boat in no time.

Suddenly, Uncle Maynard crouched to the ground.

"Shhhh!" he whispered.

William wanted to ask what he had seen, but he didn't dare speak and in the distance, just beyond the ring of light cast by the guesthouse's spotlight, he saw a shadow move. And then he saw another. And in the next second, two men with machine guns stepped into the light. They hadn't seen anything. They looked calm. Almost bored, really. And they were chatting.

Uncle Maynard began to inch backward into the young people. They followed suit, and slowly inched back as well. They were still in the darkness and in the cover of the bushes. And the guards were still some distance away. All the same, they couldn't make any noise.

They watched the guards for several minutes. One guard was talking about a car he owned, and how hard it was to keep it running these days. It was actually an extremely tedious conversation, especially if you were on a dangerous mission. The guard just kept saying things like, "I can't get the parts anymore. Nope. Can't get them anywhere. No place at all. No place." It was very frustrating. William wanted to keep moving. But there was nothing they could do. They just had to wait.

Finally, one of the guards got a call on his radio. William couldn't make out what the message said. But he heard the guard's reply.

"Okay," he said, "we'll be right there."

He put his radio on his belt and said, "Coffee?" to his partner.

"Let's go," the partner replied. And then they walked off.

William, his uncle, and Sophie waited for a second, and then Uncle Maynard said, "Let's go behind the cottage. I think we'll be all right. These guards seem relaxed. I don't think we'll have too much trouble."

Uncle Maynard stood upright and darted out onto the grass. He stopped for an instant, and then cut left to the edge of the woods. William and Sophie followed. Soon they were creeping through the darkness behind the guest cottage.

The moon was still following the western horizon, but there seemed to be less light than before. Just enough for them to see. This was good. The less light the better. And the stars were suddenly brighter. William glanced up at them and thought about how strange it was to see such a peaceful sight in the midst of all this. And then he looked down again and suddenly froze dead in his tracks. They had come around to the other side of the cottage. And there, in the distance, behind the guest cottage, beyond the lawn and through the woods, was an enormous clearing–a clearing that was being used as a landing field. There were two large helicopters. They sat motionless in the dim light of a single spotlight. But the truly terrifying sight lay just beyond the helicopters. There were three large alien aircraft, each cloaked in shadows, but with dim purple lights around their bases that faded on and off.

"I guess the aliens are here," William whispered. Uncle Maynard and Sophie were also motionless at this point.

"I guess so," Uncle Maynard said. He paused. Then he said, "Well, we expected it. Nothing surprising. So, onward!" Uncle Maynard abruptly darted away from the woods and led the group to the shadowy wall at the back of the guest cottage.

When they got to the cottage, they were still safely in the shadows. But there was a dim light coming from one of the back windows. The three crept to that window and looked in. It was hard to make out at first. But as their eyes scanned the room, and adjusted to the light, they realized what they were looking at. Five aliens were sleeping–curled up in horrible twisted green balls on the floor, as aliens frequently slept.

"I think we'd better be careful," Sophie said.

"I think you're right," Uncle Maynard replied. "But it's good that we know where at least some of them are. And that they're sleeping. Now, let's get to the barn."

21

Again, getting to the barn was tricky. It was on the other side of the Blackthorne compound, next to the caretaker's cottage. Uncle Maynard led the way. He cut back to the edge of the woods that surrounded the compound and began to follow the tree line, just barely visible in the dim moonlight.

They ran for some distance and eventually passed behind the mansion, although it was set away from the woods. It was enormous–perhaps one of the biggest houses William had ever seen–but they were moving fast and it didn't take too long to get beyond it. William noticed that there were a few lights on in the long, windowed living room that sat at the far end of the mansion. Still, the house was very quiet, and certainly no one seemed to notice the three intruders as they dashed by.

After more running, they came to the caretaker's

cottage, which was set closer to the trees. All the lights were out in this building. Our three friends came to a halt by one of the windows and looked in. They could see nothing. There was another spotlight on the top of the building, but it pointed toward the front. William, Sophie, and Uncle Maynard stayed safely in the shadows in back.

They paused for a moment, and then Uncle Maynard said, "All right, almost there," and moved away from the window.

But then he abruptly halted. He stepped back and leaned against the cottage wall. He was very out of breath. And in the next instant, he suddenly slumped to the ground.

"Uncle Maynard!" William said, a little too loudly.

"Shhhh," he replied. "I'm fine. I'm fine. Just a little unsteady. All this sneaking around isn't good for a man of my age. Strains my heart. I'll be all right in another second." Uncle Maynard then pulled several pills from his pocket and popped them in his mouth. "I'll be all right in a bit," he said again.

William and Sophie sat down beside him with their backs against the cottage wall. They were still hidden by the darkness and were safe enough there. William took off his gun and leaned it up against the wall, and then rubbed his forehead. What was next? he wondered. The grass he was sitting on was cool and smelled sweet. He looked up at the stars again as a gentle breeze grazed his cheek. Once more he was unsettled by how peaceful it was at Starling Lake and yet how frightened he was. And then, a rather remarkable thing happened.

William looked to his left, to a small stand of dark pine trees set out against the starry sky, when Sophie leaned into William and then gently propped her head against his shoulder. Her soft hair brushed against his face, and he could smell a kind of lavender perfume on her, which seemed to be the single most magnificent smell he had ever encountered. William's heart started racing–more than it had even when they were running behind the mansion. But he didn't dare move. He even tried to breathe more softly. He didn't want Sophie to shift away.

But really, he hardly knew what to make of all this, and he began thinking about how so much had changed in recent months. He actually had the idea (despite the danger and despite the hardship) that this kind of energetic and daring life was perhaps just the sort of way he ought to have been living all along, especially if one of the consequences was Sophie leaning up against him and resting her head on his shoulder. He actually thought he could stay like that all night, no matter how many men (and aliens) with guns were prowling around. But after a few more minutes, Uncle Maynard rose to his feet again. "I'm think I'm ready now," he said, although he was still having difficulty breathing.

"Are you sure you can keep going?" William asked. He said this almost without taking a breath. Again, he didn't want Sophie to shift from her position.

"Yes, yes. We've got to keep moving!" Uncle Maynard replied. "No use complaining." He tightened his scarf and then peered around the other side of the caretaker's cottage.

At last William moved slightly, and Sophie eased away from him. They stood up and came up behind Uncle Maynard to see what was ahead.

There was now only a long, broad stretch of lawn between them and the barn (or laboratory, as it now more properly was). There were lights on inside. Someone was in there. And there were faint gurgling and bubbling noises. People were at work. Still, it could be anyone. There was no telling what was going on.

22

The two buildings were actually some distance from each other. But the journey was not a difficult one. There were spotlights. But there were also long, dark shadows. And after zigzagging a bit, and then darting straight forward, William, Sophie, and Uncle Maynard soon found themselves up against the broad front wall of the enormous wooden barn.

After pausing for a moment, they began to move their way toward a low window just to the right. It didn't take long, and in about ten seconds, William, Sophie, and Uncle Maynard were peering in on quite an astonishing sight.

In front of them was an enormous room that looked like a sort of alien hospital. There were several rows of aliens on double-sized white beds. They had tubes running in and out of them. They were hooked up to various electric monitors. And they looked very, very sick. Their skin was blotchy and discolored. They were extremely thin. Their tentacles seemed weak and lifeless. And they all trembled as they slept.

There were also computer screens everywhere, with X-ray images on them. And at the far end, there were several humans in white lab coats, sitting at computers and looking at strange test tubes and stacks of red dishes.

It was all very, very impressive. It seemed strange that years ago this had all been a place to house animals. But now the old exterior walls were just kept around for decoration. The mayor's father had really put together a state-of-the-art lab, although he would surely have been astonished if he had lived to see it converted into some kind of alien medical center.

"I don't see them!" Sophie said at last. Her eyes were peering over the windowsill.

"Don't see who?" Uncle Maynard replied.

"My parents!" Sophie said, suddenly annoyed.

"Of course. Of course. Your parents. Are you sure?"

There were about six people in lab coats walking around.

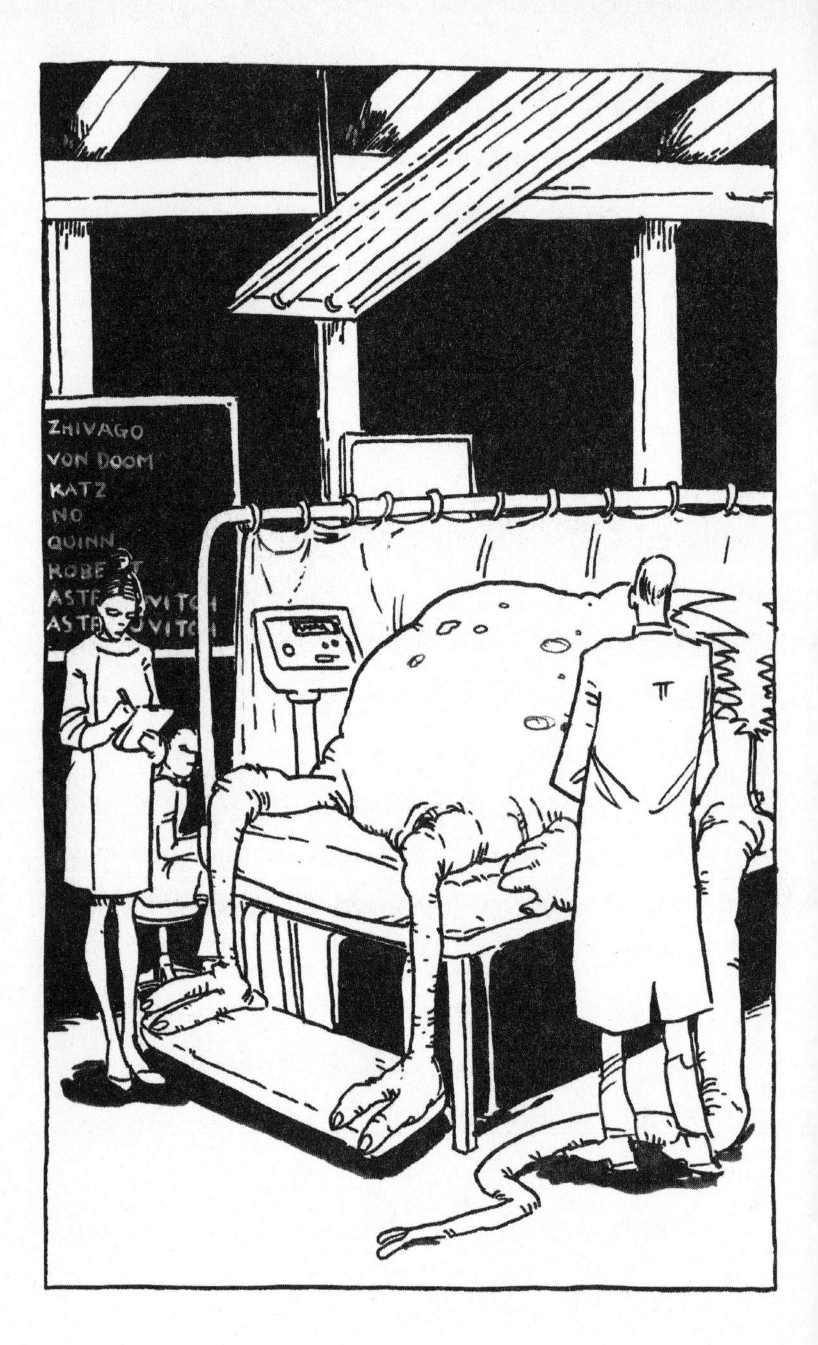
ZHIVAGO
VON DOOM
KATZ
NO
QUINN

"Yes, I'm sure," Sophie said.

They all gazed at the scene for a few more minutes, then William said, "Look to the left. At the blackboard over there. With all the names. It's a schedule. Look at the bottom."

Sophie and Uncle Maynard looked to the left, and there, at the bottom of the schedule, in the last two lines on the grid, it said "Lena Astronovitch" and then "Vladimir Astronovitch," followed by dates and times.

"That's them," Sophie whispered. "It looks like they're due to start work at seven tomorrow morning."

"Well, at least we know they haven't been eaten," Uncle Maynard said.

"Will you please stop talking about my parents being eaten!" Sophie barked.

"I said they *weren't* eaten," Uncle Maynard replied.

"I don't want you to say anything at all about my parents being eaten. Nothing. I don't want to hear you say that at all. Eaten or not eaten."

All at once, William again had a very strange feeling of liking Sophie a great deal. He was always taken with her slightly sarcastic tone. Even when she leveled it against him. But it was especially funny when she used it with Uncle Maynard.

And then William quickly came back to reality. He decided he needed to focus, to stick to the task at hand, and not think about how much he liked Sophie. They had to figure out what was next. They couldn't stand around there forever, given the fact that there were aliens and armed men running around. And where were Sophie's parents? Asleep, probably, but where?

It was at this point that William realized that something was wrong. He touched his shoulder and discovered that his gun was gone. He had left it against the wall of the caretaker's cottage. He had to go back to get it.

"Hey!" he whispered. "I've got to run back to the caretaker's house. I left my gun there."

Sophie groaned, then said, "Can we please try to keep it together, guys? This is serious here."

"I know, I know," William replied. "I'll just be a minute. See if you can spot a way in. I'll be right back."

And with that, William began darting and zigzagging back to the caretaker's cottage. It was an easy trip. All through the darkness. But when he got to the cottage, things changed very quickly. Just as he darted around the small building, he heard a voice behind him, near the barn, yell, "Hey! Who are you? What are you doing here!"

William quickly crouched down. Then he carefully peered back around the wall. There, at the barn window, Sophie and Uncle Maynard stood paralyzed in the light of a very bright flashlight. Two guards, guns drawn, were slowly stepping toward them.

"Who are you?" a guard yelled again.

William could see Sophie begin reaching down to her waist, where her gun was hanging. Then he heard a guard shout, "Don't be stupid, young lady. You won't make it."

This was good advice, William thought–both the guards had their guns pointed right at them. She never would have made it to the trigger.

In the next second, one of the guards was next to Sophie and Uncle Maynard, taking their guns from them.

23

A bright flashlight attached to the end of the guard's gun was now shining on Uncle Maynard's face. It was some distance away, but for the first time, in this bright light, William could see how exhausted Uncle Maynard really was. Of course, no one looks healthy with a flashlight shining right in his face. But Uncle Maynard seemed particularly ill.

"I'm going to ask you again," one of the guards said. "Who are you?"

And once again, there was no reply.

"Normally we'd just shoot you," the other guard said. "But an old man and a girl. Doesn't seem right. So we're doing you a favor. You might want to be nice and answer our questions. Because we could shoot you."

"We're from the neighboring house," Uncle Maynard finally said. "We're staying at the Abernathys' house."

"A little vacation, huh?" a guard said.

"Just a little vacation," Uncle Maynard replied, forcing a smile.

"What's with the guns then?" the guard asked.

"Well, perhaps you haven't noticed, but there are man-eating aliens everywhere."

"That would be a good reason to stay inside at night. Not creeping around other people's property."

"We couldn't sleep. We needed some air."

"Uh-huh," the guard said, and then turned to his partner. "Let's take them to the mayor."

"Good, take us to the mayor!" Uncle Maynard said, now more defiant. "Take us to the mayor and see what he says. Young Preston will have a lot to say about this!" Sophie remained silent during all this, although William could tell she was holding back quite a bit of fury. She didn't seem scared. She seemed extremely angry.

"So, you know the mayor?" the guard continued.

"I do indeed," Uncle Maynard replied.

"Well, good. Then you'll have lots to talk about." The guard turned to his partner and said, "Let's lock them up with the doctors while we get Mayor Walters."

"This way," the other guard said, poking Uncle Maynard in the ribs with his gun.

To William's surprise, the guard suddenly pointed his flashlight exactly in William's direction. But the guard didn't seem to see him.

"Right over there," the guard said. In the next instant, the two guards and their two prisoners were walking directly toward the caretaker's cottage.

William quickly thought about what he ought to do. But he was at a loss. In this kind of situation, he was much better at taking orders. Coming up with his own ideas was a bit harder. If he were improvising something on the violin, he might be able to manage something interesting. Freeing friends who had been captured by evil men and aliens, however, was a very different story.

William's first job, though, was to not get caught

himself. He crawled to the other side of the cottage and back into a thick patch of bushes, nearly fifteen feet away. From there, he watched as the flashlights moved closer to the cottage, darting back and forth, and occasionally flashing across Uncle Maynard and Sophie.

"Let's pick up the pace," one of the guards snapped as a flashlight shone on Uncle Maynard's face.

"All right, all right," Uncle Maynard said. "Can't you see I'm an old man? This is as fast as I can move." Sophie wasn't moving very quickly either, but her stiffness suggested that she still wanted to turn and start fighting. Fortunately, she was smart enough to do as she was told. There were guards with guns behind her, after all.

In a few more seconds, the guards and the prisoners disappeared from William's view. About the same time, lights came on in the cottage. And through the back windows (each of which had bars across them), William watched as people in bunk beds woke up and looked at the new arrivals.

William hoped that if Sophie's parents were in there, they'd play it cool when they were reunited–

if there was too much of a tearful reunion, the guards would know for sure that something was up. But you can hardly expect a daughter and her parents to keep quiet when they see each other after such an ordeal. And through the windows, William watched as two people (a bearded man and a woman with short dark hair) leapt out of their bunks and bolted toward Sophie, taking her in their arms and hugging her. And with that, Sophie's defiant and angry demeanor was gone. She hugged her parents back, nearly in tears. For whatever trouble they were all in, she was now very, very happy.

William suddenly thought about how long it had been since he had last been with his own mother and father. And in the next instant, he became even more determined to rescue his uncle, and Sophie, and her parents, and everyone else who was locked in that cottage.

24

But first, William had to wait. He could hardly break into the cottage when the two guards were still in there. And after they locked up and left, he still felt unsure of what to do. It was true he had a gun. But he couldn't use it to break through the barred windows with all the people on the other side. And who knew what else was in the cottage? William thought it wasn't unlikely that there were other guards or even man-eating aliens posted in there, although he remembered all the lights had been out when they first passed by. All the lights were out again now–the guards had shut them off–so there was no way for William to gather much information about what lay ahead.

William thought over and over about what he should do, and he slowly became more and more upset with himself for being so bad in this kind of situation. He imagined playing scales on his violin to calm himself down. But he mostly wished, just at this moment, that he had spent his time learning something more useful than a musical instrument–like archery, perhaps, or gymnastics.

But William didn't have long to think about these things. About five minutes after the guards had locked up the cottage and walked to the mansion, they returned.

William heard one of them say, "Boy, the mayor's a grump when he wakes up. You'd think we threw him in the lake."

"No kidding. But he'd be more angry if we didn't get him out of bed."

The guards disappeared in front of the small cottage, all the lights came back on, and William watched through the windows as Uncle Maynard, Sophie, and Sophie's parents were corralled together and led out of the bedroom. None of them looked happy, and Sophie in particular looked like she wanted to start throwing punches. But again, she kept her cool.

William, too, kept his head, holding his ground

in the bushes. There was no point in moving yet. But when he watched the guards lead Uncle Maynard, Sophie, and her parents back toward the mansion, he decided to follow. He wanted to make sure he knew where Sophie and his uncle were at all times. And they might need him. After all, these two prisoners were hardly valuable to the mayor. They weren't doctors or scientists. So they might well be fed to the aliens after they were questioned.

William kept a safe distance from the party ahead of him. And as they turned and went in the front door of the mansion, William went to the back.

He had to be careful, though. The lights were on in the large, windowed room that sat at one end of the mansion, and the light shined outside. It would be easier for him to be spotted.

William again found a convenient bush to hide behind. He tried to stay away from the light, but he couldn't go too far. This large, windowed room seemed to be where the activity was. In fact, just after William found his new hiding place, the mayor suddenly walked into the room. This was where William had to keep watch. No good picking a safer hiding place if he couldn't see anything.

And this was a good decision. In the next instant, the mayor took a seat behind a large desk, not far from the window, and then a large door opened and in walked Uncle Maynard, Sophie, and Sophie's parents, followed by the two guards.

25

It didn't take long for things to get heated. Although William couldn't hear anything, Uncle Maynard definitely seemed to get the ball rolling, immediately starting to yell and storm around the room, tightening his scarf, then loosening it, slamming his hand against the bookshelves, squinting and pulling at his hair, stomping his feet, and really putting on a show as he told the mayor what was on his mind.

The mayor listened patiently, barely moving as he and everyone else watched Uncle Maynard move back and forth. But at last, after nearly five minutes of Uncle Maynard's yelling, the mayor abruptly stood up, held his arms out wide, and he himself began to pace the room as he responded. Again, William could hear nothing, but it was obvious that the mayor's response was just as animated as Uncle Maynard's tirade had been. The mayor slapped his hands together, pointed into the air, beat his chest with a fist, put the palm of his hand against his forehead, and did numerous other things before finally stepping forward and gently putting his hand on Uncle Maynard's shoulder.

This final gesture was not well received, at least as far as William could tell. Uncle Maynard quickly stepped back and said something that (judging from the mayor's face) was extremely offensive. The mayor paused, went back to his desk, pressed a button, and in the next second two more guards came in. They stood silently for a moment, and then something quite surprising happened. Another door at the other side of the room opened and in walked Caldwell Jones–the man who had been on TV and with the aliens when they took away Sophie's parents. William could see that Sophie was stunned to see him (as were her parents), and now she began to yell. But one of the guards quickly grabbed her and pulled her out the other door. Uncle Maynard immediately followed, as did the rest of the guards, the mayor, the Doctors Astronovitch, and Caldwell Jones.

William wondered where they were headed, but in

the next minute, sound finally returned, as William heard them all step outside.

"If your father were alive, this would kill him," Uncle Maynard yelled, loud enough for William to easily hear from his hiding place in the bushes. "It would kill him. It would absolutely kill him!"

"Maynard, you have to understand my position."

"You will call me Mr. Bright, young man!" he replied.

"The point is, I have no choice in all this. And I can tell you that I answer to some very powerful people–or creatures, I should say. If you cause any more trouble, you won't see the end of the week."

"Are you threatening me?"

"I'm telling you the truth."

"You're threatening me!"

"You're not listening!"

The group was walking back toward the caretaker's cottage by this point, and William was doing his best to follow silently at the edge of the woods. He managed to avoid making any loud noises, although with all the screaming, it seemed that he could set off a stick of dynamite and no one would notice.

"Well, I'll tell you this," Uncle Maynard continued. "When I get back to Willoughby, I'm going to call for a public emergency meeting of the city council. If you think you can kidnap free citizens like this, you're out of your mind!"

"Well, you could do that," the mayor replied, the group now nearing the cottage. "Except that at this point, I'm afraid I can't let you leave."

"What's that? Can't let me leave?" Uncle Maynard halted.

The mayor stopped as well, and then, in a moment of silence, pulled a cigar from his left breast pocket and lit it.

"I can't let you leave," he finally said again, after several hard puffs.

"Ridiculous!" Uncle Maynard replied. "You will let us go this instant!"

"Look, you've snuck onto my land in order to destroy a very important project I have going on here. I just can't let you head back to the city to start more trouble. Anyway, it's very nice here. I suggest you learn to appreciate it, because, like I said, the people–or things–I work for are very unforgiving."

"Preston, you are to let us go immediately. Think of your father. What would he say to all this? He would tell you that you are behaving very, very badly. He would be immensely disappointed in you."

The mayor paused for a moment, looked at the ground, took a puff from his cigar, and then, suddenly, with no warning at all, stepped forward and punched Uncle Maynard right in the stomach. It was a crushing blow, and Uncle Maynard immediately dropped to the ground, gasping.

"Stop living in the past, old man!" the mayor yelled. "I'm in charge. And don't ever call me Preston again. It's Mayor Walters to you, Maynard."

The mayor stepped forward and kicked Uncle Maynard in the ribs. Then he looked up at the guards and Caldwell Jones and said, "Lock them up."

The mayor watched as Uncle Maynard was hoisted to his feet and Sophie and her parents were pushed forward.

"You heard the mayor," Jones said, smiling. "Time for bed."

William was still at the edge of the woods during all this, wondering what he should do. He had wanted to act during the whole conversation, but it was so hard to know how. He could hardly take on four guards. And the fact was that any kind of gunfight would likely injure Sophie or Uncle Maynard or the Astronovitches. And now they were being locked up again. It seemed that after things quieted down, he might be able to break into the cottage somehow, although he still didn't know how he'd manage this.

And then something happened that caused him to think very differently about the situation.

The mayor stood motionless for a moment as the prisoners were dragged around the front of the cottage. Then he looked up at the moon, which was still hovering around the horizon and casting just a bit of light on him. He stared for a moment, then took a long puff on his cigar and started pacing. At first it was just in small circles. Then he turned and walked toward the lake. And then he turned back and headed toward the woods–right to where William was now crouching in the bushes.

William expected the mayor to stop. He was clearly deep in thought. He wasn't going anywhere in particular. He was just smoking and thinking. But in his somewhat dreamy state, he was now quickly approaching William. And before William could move, he was about fifteen feet away. The lights in the windows of the bunk room were now back on as the prisoners found their way to where they would be sleeping, so William was nearly in the light. If the mayor came much closer, he'd be able to spot William.

William thought very carefully for a moment and then came up with something of a plan. As the mayor walked forward, still smoking his cigar and glancing up at the moon, William suddenly stood up. Light from the cottage now shone across William's face and shoulders. And as the mayor looked down from the sky and directly in front of him, William raised the gun into the light as well.

"Stop where you are," William said quietly.

The mayor simply took another puff on his cigar and smiled. He took another step forward.

"Stop where you are," William said again.

But the mayor did not stop. He kept stepping closer. Finally, he spoke: "Son, you don't want to use that on me. I'm your friend. Now put it down, and let's talk this over."

William turned the setting on his gun down all the way–it would just stun him. Still, he wasn't sure what to do. He had to do something though. And the fact was that he was suddenly possessed with a kind of wild anger. Images of the mayor punching his uncle raced through his mind and made him more and more furious.

Again, the mayor took a step forward, now with one of his arms outstretched. "Give me the gun, son," he said.

Considering the matter no more, William drew the gun back and (somewhat irrationally) swung it forward, striking the mayor right across his right kneecap with the gun's hard barrel, sending the mayor crashing to the ground in agony. Then William sent a bright, blistering electric pulse right into the mayor's other leg. And then another. And then another after that.

"Stop!" the mayor finally yelled. "Stop!"

William suddenly felt slightly guilty. The mayor was a bad man. There was no question about that. But it really was not in William's nature to hurt people. Still, he had to look tough. If he looked weak now, he'd be locked up in the caretaker's cottage in no time.

The unfortunate thing about the mayor's injuries, however, was that he was now making lots of noise. And in the next minute, Caldwell Jones and the four guards were approaching, flashlights and lanterns swinging in all directions, and lots of confused chatter about what they had heard.

As the flashlights pointed at him and the mayor, William ratcheted up the dial on his gun and yelled, "Drop your guns, and don't come any closer."

Jones and the guards stopped for a moment. None of their guns was pointed at William. In the end, it wouldn't have been too difficult for them to shoot him. But the mayor would surely be injured if there was a gunfight. The guards shined their flashlights across William, and across the mayor, who was still on the ground, clutching his kneecap. The lanterns were close enough that they, too, spread some light across the scene. The guards paused for a moment, and then started to inch forward again.

William didn't repeat himself. Instead, he let go with another sizzling bolt of electricity right into the mayor's thigh. In the long run, such a shock was harmless. But in the short run, it was obviously very painful. The mayor immediately started yelling even louder. "Back off you idiots!" he yelled. "Get away from me!"

The guards continued to hesitate as William coaxed the dial forward a little more. "Stop where you are and drop your guns," William said. "I mean it. The next shock is going to be for real."

The guards paused, but in the midst of his groaning, the mayor again yelled, "Drop them you dopes! Drop them! We'll talk. We'll talk this over. Don't worry. Just do what he says."

Jones and the guards dropped their guns, and William surveyed the scene, wondering just what he ought to do next.

It seemed like several hours to William as he stood before Caldwell Jones and the four disarmed guards and a now injured mayor. William had never been in anything like this sort of situation, and he didn't quite know how to handle it. At last, however, he came to a decision.

"Who has the keys to the cottage?" he said.

The guards paused, unsure of what to do, but William realized that there was no time to wait. He inched the gun's charge down and zapped the mayor.

"Tell him who has the keys!" the mayor yelled in agony.

"I do, I do," one of the guards said. He reached to his belt and detached a ring of keys.

"Two of you," William said to the guards. "Come here and pick up the mayor."

They stepped forward and helped the mayor to his feet. He could stand, but his legs were shaking.

"All right," William said. "We're going to walk around to the front door and let everyone out."

"You're just making things harder on yourself," the mayor gasped. "Give up, and I'll make sure you stay alive. Otherwise, you'll be fed to the aliens before the sun rises."

William thought about shooting the mayor again, but decided against it. He needed the mayor to be able to walk. "We'll take our chances," he said.

William followed the guards around to the front of the cottage. Jones had taken the keys and was in the lead, with two guards by his side. Following them was the mayor and the two guards helping him. And then came William, his gun raised and pointed at the backs of the men ahead.

In another second, Jones was at the front door and opening the lock. "Go slowly," William said. "I promise you I'll shoot the mayor again."

"Go slowly! Go slowly!" the mayor yelled, still in pain.

It didn't take long to get through the first door, flip on the lights, and step into the entry hall. In another moment, Jones was unlocking the door to the bunk room, and soon William was surrounded by Sophie, Uncle Maynard, the Doctors Astro-novitch, and several other grateful doctors he had not yet met.

"William!" Sophie yelled, hugging him tightly. "I knew you'd find a way to rescue us."

"Yes, well done, William," Uncle Maynard added, although his voice was weak. The mayor's punch had obviously injured him, and in the harsh light of the bunk room, his skin looked a grayish green color and his eyes were bloodshot. He looked very tired.

Still, William didn't have time to consider this. He and the others quickly took the guards' hand-cuffs and began locking them to the metal frames of the bunk beds. They also took their radios, so they wouldn't be able to contact anyone when they made their escape.

"Let's hold on to the mayor," William suggested, as one of the doctors pulled him toward a bunk. "I think it might help to have a hostage."

Everyone seemed to agree to this idea, but they were all suddenly distracted by Sophie, who had stepped toward the now-locked-up Caldwell Jones.

"Not so tough now, are you?" she said, kicking him in the leg.

Jones yelled in pain, but he also seemed to be smiling. "I give you fifteen minutes before the aliens eat you, young lady," he said.

Sophie immediately kicked him again, and then punched him in the stomach, causing him to quickly lurch forward. But he was still smiling.

Sophie turned and said, "OK. I'm ready to go now."

"Let's get going then," Uncle Maynard said. William pushed the mayor forward and then said to Jones and the guards, "If any of you yell for help, the mayor will pay for it."

"No yelling!" the mayor barked, although he was

now a little less wobbly than he had been a few minutes earlier.

It was possible that no one would find the handcuffed guards till the morning. William, however, was pretty sure they'd start yelling once they figured that the fugitives were out of earshot. All the same, that would give them a little lead time.

After locking the door to the bunk room, the group gathered in the front hall to discuss plans. It was quickly (and quietly) decided that they should split into two groups. Besides Doctor and Doctor Astronovitch, there were six other scientists. Too many for the boat. And anyway, two groups would make it harder for the aliens and the mayor's men to follow them.

A member of this group of six scientists went back into the bunk room and soon returned with the car keys of one of the guards.

"We'll go out on the road," she said as she unlocked the door. "I don't think anyone expected a rescue party, so it shouldn't be too hard."

"We'll go back by boat, the way we came," Uncle Maynard said. "And we'll take the mayor with us.

How does that sound, William?"

"It sounds like a good plan," William replied.

At this point, they quietly left the cottage and went around to the back, now shrouded again in the dim shadows cast by the moon. There they said their good-byes, the Doctors Astronovitch hugging each of the other scientists. It was a rather moving farewell–they all seemed to have been old friends from the university–but the most interesting part was when Vladimir Astronovitch said, "To think, all this over chicken pox!"

"What's that?" Uncle Maynard said.

"Chicken pox," another doctor said–an oldish man with a long gray beard. "That's what these aliens are suffering from. Chicken pox. Tears right through their bodies. A very deadly thing for them."

It was astonishing news, but they didn't have time to discuss this puzzling piece of information. They had to get moving. In the next instant, the two groups said another quick farewell and went their separate ways. Before long, William and his party were once again sneaking along the edge of the woods, back toward the electric boat.

This trip was not long. William kept close behind the mayor, prodding him every so often with his gun to let him know that electric shock was still a threat, the whole while Uncle Maynard muttering to himself about what he had just learned from the doctors. "Chicken pox. Imagine!" he mumbled, over and over. "Of all things! Chicken pox!"

The group kept a lookout for guards as they moved, but didn't spot any until they came close to the guesthouse. There, they saw three armed men standing in a circle, talking and laughing. They were some ways off, and the group quickly ducked behind a large bush.

"Make sure you keep quiet," William whispered to the mayor.

The mayor just groaned and muttered something about the dismal quality of his security team. In a few minutes, the three guards turned and headed back toward the mansion. After it looked safe, the escapees continued on toward the boat.

It took another five minutes and a few sudden stops–whenever they thought they spotted something. But they made it, and it seemed at this point that they were actually much closer to escaping. The boat was still there, waiting for them. All they had to do now was make it back across the lake before the locked-up guards were discovered and they sent out a search party. This, however, would be no small feat.

27

It took a few minutes for the group of escapees (and the captive mayor) to clamber aboard the boat. Still, it happened without incident, and once they were all in, Uncle Maynard started the electric motor and turned the boat back toward the Finneman estate.

Uncle Maynard followed the shore again to find his way. It was still dark, and the shadowy shoreline was the easiest guide. The group was silent at first, except for the mayor, who was groaning and rubbing his right thigh where the largest dose of electricity had entered him. Still, the momentary silence was something of a relief. William and Sophie were seated next to each other. Across from them were the Doctors Astronovitch. The mayor was in the front. And Uncle Maynard sat in the back, at the wheel. They were now all a boat trip away from reclaiming their freedom.

But there was much that still threatened our heroes (and the mayor!). And after just a few minutes of silent relief, several very bright lights suddenly appeared back at Blackthorne Lodge. At first it wasn't clear what part of the compound could possibly be so bright. But the question was soon answered. The lights began to rise into the air. They were alien aircraft.

"They're coming to look for us!" Sophie yelled.

"It's a big lake," Uncle Maynard replied. "We've still got a good shot at making it."

"They'll find you," the mayor groaned. "No question about that." William leaned forward and jammed the barrel of his gun up against the mayor's rib cage. The mayor quickly closed his mouth. Still, it did seem like he might be right.

Suddenly, the aircraft shot away from them, away from the lake.

There was a moment of confused silence, and then Sophie's mother finally said, "They don't know we're escaping by water. They must be going after the others on the road."

Sophie and William looked at each other, but they and everyone else remained silent because this did, indeed, seem to be what was happening. The lights turned into a kind of milky haze, as the aircraft moved over the trees. They could hear the faint whistling as the aircraft moved. And the milky light continued to vibrate and shift above the treetops. The aircraft seemed to be moving fast and darting to the left and the right. Uncle Maynard kept the boat going toward the Finneman estate. But he looked back every few seconds to see what was happening.

All at once, in the distance, beyond Blackthorne Lodge, there were several loud explosions. They came on one after another. And a bright fiery light now rose up from the tree line.

"What is that?" Sophie yelled.

No one replied.

"What is that?" Sophie yelled again.

Again, no one said anything, although everyone (including Sophie) appeared to have some idea that the other scientists had just been attacked by the aliens. If they were lucky, they were captured. But the less appealing possibility seemed more likely.

"We're all going to be fine!" Uncle Maynard finally exclaimed, pushing the boat full steam ahead. "I'm not letting any aliens catch up with us."

But the explosions continued, and the fiery light got brighter, and there was again the impression amongst the party that they would not be fine at all. No one seconded Uncle Maynard's declaration or said anything that might indicate any sort of optimism. There was just nervous silence. In fact, people were so lost in thought over the problems that they now faced, that they failed to pay attention to one of their chief concerns. They were all looking back at the explosions. Suddenly, they heard a loud splash. They all looked toward the water, and in the dim moonlight, they watched the mayor swimming for the shore.

"Oh, for goodness' sake!" Uncle Maynard yelled

several times, as he swiftly changed directions, steering the boat toward the mayor. The electric boat was certainly faster than the fleeing Preston Walters. But they were close to land, and the mayor was very near the shore. Uncle Maynard gunned the boat forward for a moment. But the mayor had already begun to clamber up on land. At this moment, William decided to let off a burst of his gun. But it only hit a tree, as the mayor scrambled into the woods.

"For goodness' sake!" Uncle Maynard said again. Then he quickly turned back in the direction of the Finneman estate. "It will be too hard to catch him!" Uncle Maynard yelled. "Now we just need to get home as quickly as possible. It will take the mayor about five minutes to run along the shore to the compound. Too quick. Not good for us. Not good!"

This was echoed by the mayor, who stopped for a moment, just long enough to yell some extremely vulgar threats at the group, concluding with the statement that they would all soon be killed. "I'm telling them not to take prisoners," he screamed. "You're all going to die!"

"Well, he's wrong about that," Uncle Maynard

replied. But no one spoke up in agreement. There was only a thick and worried silence. William looked back and stared at the gentle waves trailing behind the boat. The beauty of the motor was that it was quiet. You could barely hear anything. It was perfect for sneaking up on a place or even cruising around while drinking cocktails. But at that moment, William would have preferred a great roaring noise coming from the back, and a boat that shot across the water behind a giant, ugly engine. They were now paying the price for such a silent, graceful vessel.

Minute by minute, time crept by, mostly in silence. William desperately hoped they could make it to the car before the mayor got back to his estate and alerted the aliens. They were now not far from the Finneman estate. Less than ten minutes. They'd dock. They'd run to the car, make it back to grab the violins and leftover lasagna, and hit the road. This, of course, would lead to another set of problems. But once they were off the lake and into their car, they would be at least a little safer. The alien aircraft were still far off.

"I'm sure they think we're on the road as well,"

Uncle Maynard said. "With the other scientists."

"So long as the mayor hasn't gotten back," Sophie's father replied.

But just as he said this, bright lights reappeared on the horizon. They hovered motionless for a moment. Then they shifted positions. And then they started swooping forward over the lake.

"I think that perhaps Preston has made it back," Uncle Maynard said, trying to squeeze every bit of power out of the boat. They were getting closer to the Finnemans' dock, but the alien aircraft were now covering the lake at great speeds. They had huge lights beaming down on the water. And they took a kind of serpentine pattern, following the shoreline–the route the fugitives had just taken.

"I think Preston definitely made it back!" Uncle Maynard said.

"Go to the center of the lake!" Sophie's mother suddenly yelled. "They think we're along the shore."

Uncle Maynard hesitated. Then he veered left toward the lake's center and held this course for nearly twenty seconds. But the aliens were gaining ground. And it didn't look like their elegant electric boat would make it out of their flight line. The aliens were definitely going to catch them, even if they did get closer to the center.

Suddenly, Uncle Maynard turned back toward the shore.

"I have another idea!" he yelled. "There's a canvas top to this boat. It's rolled up behind the backseat." (Again, the electric cocktail boat had a kind of wooden canopy that could support a waterproof canvas top.) "Get it out and put it on."

William and Sophie did as they were told, although the Doctors Astronovitch hesitated.

"I know what I'm doing!" Uncle Maynard yelled. "We don't have much time."

The doctors paused again, but in another second, they were snapping and tying the dark canvas top to the wooden frame. It also occurred to William that this top wasn't going to help them very much. But his uncle seemed to have a plan. And what else were they going to do?

At this point, Uncle Maynard brought the boat along the shore. When they were about ten feet away from land, he yelled, "Everyone out! Get back into the woods. Away from the lake where the aliens might spot you. William, bring that gun to me first."

William stepped forward with the aliens' electric-beam gun as Sophie and her parents jumped into the shallow water and waded ashore. The boat continued to move away from the alien aircraft and now away from the Astronovitches.

Uncle Maynard took the gun from William and said, "Get to shore now. I'll be there in a minute."

At this William halted. His uncle's voice sounded very thin, like he was very sick and completely exhausted–almost like he was having difficulty breathing. William didn't want to leave him. But Uncle Maynard yelled (as best he could), "Get on with it, William! I'll just be a minute."

William hesitated again and then jumped off. He found himself waist-deep in the water and wading, now even farther down the shore from the Astronovitches. He headed toward land but looked back to watch his uncle.

Uncle Maynard was looking down for a moment. Then he suddenly pulled the throttle back all the way. The boat lurched forward. Next, Uncle Maynard jammed the gun behind the wheel, pointing it toward the alien aircraft. He took off his scarf and forced it into the gun's trigger loop. The gun immediately started shooting. Electric bursts flew in the direction of the aircraft, although they were still far out of range.

Uncle Maynard looked up at the alien aircraft for a moment. Then he looked at the shore and jumped in the lake.

William watched as the boat sped off into the center of Starling Lake. The gun's electric beam was shooting high, although it wasn't coming near the aircraft. In fact, it stood no chance of actually damaging any of the aliens. But it caught their attention. It was a perfect decoy. With the dark canopy, and the firing gun, it looked exactly like the fugitives were still on board and firing at the aliens. And in another second, the aircraft were speeding directly toward the boat.

William looked ahead at Uncle Maynard. He was now slowly swimming toward him and not that far from shore as the boat sped farther and farther away. In the next second, Uncle Maynard reached shallow water and was finally able to stand. He followed William onto the land just as the alien aircraft

converged on the boat. Their lights shined down but couldn't see inside. The canopy was covering the interior. In the next moment, each of the aircraft opened fire, launching fiery bombs at the Finnemans' electric boat. There was a huge explosion, and the boat was blown to pieces. Thousands of tiny wooden splinters shot into the air beneath an enormous fireball.

William and Uncle Maynard stood silently together onshore, just behind some scrub oaks at the edge of the woods, looking at the fire in front of them. William could hardly catch his breath. Finally, Uncle Maynard said, "Well, they think we're dead now. Let's get to the others."

The aircraft remained hovering above the explosion, although it was clear to William that they wouldn't find much. If they'd been on the boat, they would have been entirely destroyed, so there wasn't a lot for the aliens to even look for. And as William and his uncle stepped into the darkness of the woods, he concluded that the aliens had to be confident that they had killed them.

"I really think we might be safe now," Uncle Maynard said as they made it farther into the trees that rimmed the shoreline. The first signs of dawn had begun to arrive. Uncle Maynard seemed happy to William, but his voice was still very unsteady and weak.

"They're sure we're dead now," Uncle Maynard said again, now coming to a halt. "Who could survive an attack like that? They won't be coming after us. But I think you and I may have to head north at this point. Can't go back to Willoughby now. I think we made the mayor very angry. Especially you, my boy."

Uncle Maynard laughed.

"They're sure we're dead now," he said again.

And then, suddenly, Uncle Maynard collapsed on the ground.

William was confused for an instant, but then quickly dropped to his knees. "Uncle Maynard!" he yelled.

Uncle Maynard was slumped into a kind of ball and struggling to speak. Finally, he said weakly, "I'm all right, William. I'm all right. Now, let's get a move on. Get the others. We need to get to our car. To head north. To the Northern Empire."

But Uncle Maynard barely moved as he said this.

"What's the matter?" William said, helping Uncle Maynard to lie down properly. "Are you hurt?"

"I'm afraid I'm having a hard time moving," he replied, now on his back. "I know I fuss quite a bit about it, but I'm thinking that my heart isn't doing very well. In fact, I'd say that at this moment, it hurts a great deal. All that activity just then. Not good for me. I'm not supposed to swim. Or run. Or get punched by psychotic mayors."

William had heard Uncle Maynard's complaints before. But he understood very clearly that this was different. William began calling for the Astro-novitch family, although he could see in the first sliver of dawn light that they were now already weaving between the trees and running toward them.

"It's all right, William," Uncle Maynard said. "This will pass. I'll be up in no time."

But now William started yelling with even greater desperation. "Quickly!" he yelled. "Run faster!"

In another minute, Sophie and her parents arrived. "What happened?" Sophie gasped.

"He says it's his heart," William replied. William stood up and moved back to let the doctors come closer. "Tell them how it hurts, Uncle Maynard," William said.

But Uncle Maynard didn't respond. He was now motionless. It was still dark, but the dawn sun was spreading a dim light across his face. And what William saw brought a terrible lump to his throat. As he stood over his uncle, he could see that his face was taught and gray. His eyes were clenched tight. And his mouth and lips seemed to have lost all their life.

Suddenly Sophie's mother yelled, "His heart has stopped! And he's not breathing." She quickly straddled Uncle Maynard, put her hands on his chest, and started pushing.

"Has he had problems with his heart before?" Sophie's father yelled.

"For years," William replied, his throat now dry and aching. "He's had heart attacks before. And surgery."

Sophie's mother continued to push on Uncle Maynard's chest. It was a rhythmic pressure. And then, after a pause, she brought her fist crashing onto his ribs. Then she started pressing again with both hands. She did this over and over, as Sophie's father held Uncle Maynard's wrist and pressed his fingers up against Uncle Maynard's neck, searching for a pulse. It lasted for some time. Forever, it seemed to William. And as he tried to grasp what was happening before him, he found that tears were streaming down his face and he was unable to speak. He wanted to yell something–to yell at Sophie's mother to save his uncle. But he couldn't open his mouth. He couldn't move at all. He just stood there, looking down and crying.

And then something happened. Sophie's father shouted, "It's started again!"

William stepped forward. He paused, then asked, "Will he be all right?"

"We'll save him," Sophie's mother replied, and then quickly leaned forward and put her mouth on Uncle Maynard's.

"Mouth-to-mouth resuscitation," Sophie's father said to William. "We need to get him breathing again."

And again, it seemed to last forever. It was a terrible thing to see Uncle Maynard being handled like this. He was like a stuffed animal being cast about by a young child. And as William looked down on all this, he became aware of the fact that he was now crying even harder–desperately and without any ability to stop himself.

But there was still hope. William still had hope.

And then, just as suddenly, Uncle Maynard started breathing again.

At first it was strange, halting gasps. But it was breathing. Sophie's mother pulled away. She elevated his legs and put her jacket under his head.

William dropped to his knees next to his uncle. He was still crying. Uncle Maynard continued gasping, and his face was still drawn and tight.

"Uncle Maynard," William said. "Can you hear me? You're going to be all right."

"He won't be able to respond," Sophie's father said.

But Uncle Maynard did respond.

His voice was barely audible, but William was right next to his mouth and he could well make out what his uncle said. "We've got to get going, William," he whispered. "Can't wait around here forever. We've got to press on. The sooner we get to the Northern Empire, the better. We've got to get started."

Uncle Maynard struggled for a moment, and then paused again.

He lay still, then leaned forward very slightly.

William's head was next to his uncle's, and he could tell he wanted to say something else.

William moved even closer.

His uncle paused, then whispered, "Oh, William, I'm so sorry that you've had to see all this. I'm so sorry for it all."

Uncle Maynard leaned forward again, just slightly, and with a small tremor. Then his head slipped back against the jacket Sophie's mother had put there. His mouth closed again, and his eyes shut tightly.

William watched for a moment, still crouching

next to his uncle. He was still breathing. But the breathing was very weak.

William wasn't sure what was happening, and he began to wonder how they were going to carry him out. Sophie's father was on his knees, holding his uncle's wrist, still taking his pulse. But he wasn't doing much more than that. There wasn't a lot they could do out there in the woods. They had to get him to a hospital, although this was a tall order in an age where aliens had destroyed much of the earth. They could bring his uncle back to the mayor's. They had medical facilities there. William would take whatever punishment the mayor had in store for him, if he'd just help his uncle. There was nothing else for it. That's what they'd have to do.

And then, William, still crouching above his uncle, looked down and saw that his uncle had stopped breathing again. "He's not breathing!" he yelled immediately. He quickly stood up and pushed Sophie's mother toward his uncle. She gave William a desperate look and bent down again to give Uncle Maynard mouth-to-mouth resuscitation. As she started, Sophie's father leaned forward, still holding

Uncle Maynard's wrist, and said, "His heart has almost stopped. It's so weak."

Sophie's mother kept giving Uncle Maynard mouth-to-mouth. But she seemed to be more desperate now.

And then Sophie's father said, "It's stopped."

Sophie's mother climbed back on Uncle Maynard's chest and brought her fist down hard. Then she started pressing. Sophie's father continued to hold Uncle Maynard's wrist.

Sophie was standing next to William, and she took his hand and squeezed it hard. William just stared at the scene in disbelief. Sophie's mother continued working. Over and over, she pressed against his heart with the same strange rhythm. For several minutes she continued without ceasing. But this time, his uncle's heart did not start to beat again. This time, Sophie's mother finally leaned back and simply stopped.

She looked up at William. It was a strange look, one that William would never forget. It was a strange kind of desperation and helplessness that William felt he had seen before, when his parents were sick. And then, finally, Sophie's mother turned her eyes down to his uncle, and then to the ground beside him, and said, "I'm so sorry, William."

"I can't believe it," William finally choked out.

"I'm so sorry," Sophie's mother said again.

Sophie's arms were now around William's shoulders as his tears started coming. He was still unable to quite grasp what had happened. And then Sophie's mother and father were hugging him too. But despite these people who were now holding William tightly in their arms, William suddenly felt very, very alone in the world.

28

Death is a puzzle to almost everyone. And although all human cultures have fairly complex guidelines about what to do once a person has died, these guidelines rarely make much sense in the larger scheme of things (even if you absolutely believe in an afterlife, as many people do). And when it's you that's lost someone–when it's your grandmother, or brother, or uncle who's died–it's almost impossible to conceive of what's happened, let alone what to actually do.

And during the many years that followed this terrible September dawn, in the many times that William would recall this moment, he would continue to puzzle over what actually occurred after he watched his uncle die. It was like the events happened to someone else. He remembered the details, but the deeper memory, the feelings, were vague and distant.

But this is what happened. In the next moments,

in the dim light, William found himself carrying Uncle Maynard's body with the Astronovitch family along the wooded shore of Starling Lake. The body was light–lighter than William had imagined–and with four people to carry it, it didn't slow them down very much. William had insisted–he had insisted that they take the body. He wasn't going to leave his uncle there. He wanted to bury him. Properly. In the orchard next to his cottage, where William had learned to play the violin with his uncle and his uncle had played the violin as a boy. It was true that burying Uncle Maynard would take some time. The Doctors Astronovitch had said this to him. And there was the safety of the living to think of. They had to get on the road as soon as possible. But William would not leave his uncle. They had enough time. They had time to bury his uncle. The aliens thought they were dead.

And in fifteen minutes, they were passing through the Finneman estate, by the Finnemans' boathouse, and behind their home, and soon they found their way to Uncle Maynard's car, still parked beside the large bushes. And before long, William found himself in the backseat, sitting in the middle, with Sophie on one side and the body of his uncle on the other.

The drive to Uncle Maynard's cottage was short. The previous night, in the dark, with the half-covered

headlights and the entire journey still ahead of them, the trip had seemed endless. That morning it passed quickly. William remembered Uncle Maynard talking about what they would find at the mayor's mansion and how he was sure that they'd be able to do something to help Sophie's parents. But the events now all seemed so confusing. It was just so impossible to understand how his uncle could have died when their rescue had been so successful.

And soon they were back at Uncle Maynard's cottage–William and the Astronovitch family. They found shovels in the toolshed out back, and before long they were walking through the orchard, searching for a place to bury Uncle Maynard. They found a spot between two large apple trees–trees that looked much older than the rest. They were far enough apart that their roots wouldn't be a problem, and without much discussion, William and the Astronovitches began to dig. It was fall, and the apples were just about ripe, and William again thought how puzzling it was to be in such a beautiful place and yet feel so alone. Even Sophie seemed very distant to him now.

They dug for a while, two at a time, each taking turns. They managed to dig down about three feet before the hard clay made it too difficult to go any farther. Three feet was enough, William said. They had to get going.

There wasn't much to do after that. They went back to the cottage and got Uncle Maynard's body, and then brought it to the grave. William also brought Uncle Maynard's violin, thinking he might bury it with him. But the violin had belonged to Uncle Maynard's grandfather, and as they walked through the orchard, William decided that his uncle would want him to keep it.

And then they had to lay the body in the grave.

And then William became very aware that he was about to say good-bye.

His uncle was laid in the grave.

And now they had to cover him.

William took the shovel and heaped the first dirt across his uncle's body. The others joined in, and soon William watched as his uncle's hands and legs disappeared beneath the reddish brown earth. They were still shoveling two at a time. William paused for a moment and looked down at his uncle's face, and before long, this, too, disappeared.

At this point, William picked up his uncle's violin and played a short nocturne that was a favorite of Uncle Maynard's. He looked down as he began to play and saw that his uncle's body was now gone beneath the earth. And as William came to the end of the nocturne, he realized that it was time to go. He didn't quite know what to do. He didn't quite know how to leave his uncle. He had stopped playing and was now staring straight down at the grave. Then, finally, imagining his uncle telling him to carry on, to get moving before it was too late, William said, "I think we should probably leave now."

And then he turned and headed back to the cottage, now crying without reprieve and still wondering how this happened, how his uncle could really be dead.

29

There were too many decisions to be made at that moment. And without his uncle to guide him, William hardly knew where to begin.

But he was sure of one thing. It first occurred to him as he was carrying his uncle's body through the woods along Starling Lake, and by the time he was digging his uncle's grave, it was already decided.

He was not going north to the Northern Empire.

Not yet.

He was first going to Great Harbor, to find his brother.

It hardly seemed like a good decision. On almost all points, in fact, it was a very bad decision. But William was quickly running out of people he was close to, and his brother seemed to be the last person on earth that William was connected to by blood—if his brother was even still alive.

He tried to explain this to Sophie and her parents, but they told him that he was making a terrible mistake.

"You need to wait," Sophie's father said, scratching his gray beard. "See how things progress in the next few months. Who knows how long the aliens will survive here?"

"I just can't go north," William said. "Not yet. I've got to go to Great Harbor. I don't have any choice."

It was a strange kind of moment. The Astronovitches were adults. And William was just a young person. And if these had been normal times, he would have done what he was told. But things were very different now. William had spent the past two days shooting aliens, rescuing scientists, and saying good-bye to the most important person in his life. It seemed that normal notions of the role of a young person no longer applied. And the truth was that the Doctors Astronovitch seemed to recognize this as well. They said he was taking too much of a risk. They told William that the journey was long and treacherous, and that it wouldn't help his brother if he got killed on the way. But Sophie's mother finally said, "But, of course, it's your decision."

William paused, almost out of politeness, as though he was making an effort to think through their advice. But his mind was made up. After a few more seconds, he said, "I have to go to Great Harbor. I'll make it to the Northern Empire eventually. But I've got to find my brother first."

And then William looked at Sophie, and for a moment he recalled the previous day, waking up in his uncle's house to find him arguing with her about how to chop onions. It seemed so distant at this point, even though it was only a day ago. And then William started to cry again, and as he wiped his eyes and tried to stop, he wondered how long this embarrassing tendency was going to last. He wanted to look tough. He liked Sophie a great deal, and he wanted to look strong.

Sophie just stepped forward and put her arms around William.

"I'm so sorry, William," she said. "You and your uncle did so much for me. I don't know how I'll ever thank you."

William didn't reply, but for a moment he did

wonder if he shouldn't, in fact, go north with them. But then he pulled away, forced himself to stop crying, and said, "We should all really get going."

Still scratching his beard, Sophie's father said, "Yes, I think you're right. We should all get going."

30

In the next twenty minutes, William and the Astronovitches packed up. William decided he should take the blue truck and give the car to the Astronovitches–it was better for three people. Each took enough food to last for about a week. The frozen lasagnas would melt quickly enough, but Uncle Maynard's cottage was well stocked with crackers and canned soup, and they took whatever looked like it would last. And water. They filled every jug there was with water and packed that as well. After that, there wasn't too much to take. They grabbed some old maps. They took the flashlights. They took blankets from Uncle Maynard's linen closet. And they took whatever else looked like it might be of some use on what were bound to be very difficult journeys.

And then William packed his violin. He actually had two violins at this point–his uncle's and his own.

But as they were saying good-bye, William stepped forward with his uncle's violin and gave it to Sophie.

"You can keep this for me," he said. "You'll probably be in a safer place than I will. So it's better if you keep it. I can even teach you how to play when I meet up with you again." William had more to say, but in the next moment, his mouth was buried in Sophie's shoulder, and she was hugging him tightly.

"I'll take good care of it," she said, now crying herself. "I promise. And I'll see you soon."

As William got into the truck, it occurred to him again that maybe he was making a mistake. Maybe he should wait. Maybe he should go north with the Astronovitches. After all, he barely even knew how to drive. He looked around to find the place to stick the key, and then he suddenly felt another crushing sense of loss because he couldn't ask his uncle for help. It was just such a hard thing to understand—he couldn't believe that his uncle was gone. Only a few hours ago they had been crossing Starling Lake together. And now he was dead.

But William eventually found the keyhole, and started the engine, and turned the wheel to guide the old truck onto the grass-covered driveway. Then he looked in the rearview mirror and saw Sophie and her parents now pulling behind him in Uncle Maynard's car. He'd eventually make it to the Northern Empire. He knew that.

31

Many years later, when he was a grown man and the world had gone through many, many more changes, William often recalled one more event that happened on that day.

Sometime after he said good-bye—after the Astro-novitches had pulled onto the road heading north and left him to continue alone on his long trip to the coast—William pulled off at the side of the road, about an hour into his journey, to look at an old bridge that he and his uncle had visited when he was younger. They had come to the cottage the week after his brother had run away, and Uncle Maynard had taken William on a drive through the country. They had stopped at the bridge and were soon talking about what William's future might look like. This was long before anyone had any idea that there were aliens headed for Planet Earth, and Uncle Maynard

was trying to help William understand that there would eventually come a time, when he was older, that he wouldn't have to listen to mean-spirited stepparents and unkind teachers and the numerous other adults that seemed to enjoy making things so miserable for him. And when that time came, Uncle Maynard assured William over and over, he would surely see his older brother again.

"He isn't someone you've lost, William," Uncle Maynard said. "It's not like your parents. When you're old enough, you can go to Great Harbor and live on the beach for all anyone will care. You'll be free to do exactly as you like."

William sat in the truck by the bridge for nearly an hour, thinking about this. He was parked under a tree and feeling very strange about all that was ahead of him. And the truth is that the memories of his uncle seemed so painful now that he had a hard time thinking about it all. But he did anyway, and he wondered if what his uncle had told him had finally come true. He was alone and could do as he pleased. The trip ahead was going to be difficult. William knew that. All the same, he did feel just a glimmer of freedom. His mind was still tortured by what had happened that morning. There was no question about that. But it was a clear fall day. And the sun was unusually warm for late September. And if William hadn't known that the world was on the brink of dying out completely, he never would have suspected anything was wrong from what he saw in front of him—the trees, and the small brook, and the old bridge that had somehow survived for so many years.

Still, he couldn't sit there forever thinking about it all. He had to keep moving. He wasn't sure he was any safer on the road than under the tree. But at least he would be covering ground. He rubbed his eyes, looked back at the bridge, and then started up the truck and pulled back on the road, still thinking about what his uncle had told him, and now hoping that he would soon find himself in the company of his brother in the city of Great Harbor.

WATCH FOR

ALiEN BLOODBATH

CHRONiCLES of the FiRST INVASiON • Book Two

What horrors await William on his journey
across a planet devastated by man-eating aliens?

Will he find his brother?

Will he fall prey to a horde
of marauding bandits?

Will he be devoured by a drooling
creature from outer space?

All this and more in the exciting follow up to *Alien Feast*!